DIAMONDS AND SECRETS

By

MICHELLE B. HARRIS

**With love to my dear family: Amy and Joshua, Patricia and Jamie,
And my supportive and wonderful friends...**

"If diamonds could speak about their past?..."
Michelle B. Harris

Aside the references to true historical events in this novel, the characters detailed are fictitious. Any resemblance to real persons, living or dead is absolutely coincidental.

1

Chapter 1

The young woman held her baby close. The station at Oxford Circus was crowded with commuters and shoppers. The mother was oblivious to the noise; she just wanted to hear the approaching train so she could jump.

The baby started to cry; the mother was mumbling nonsense. Immersed within an intense, personal conflict she was sweating profusely. The train's headlights could be seen as it entered the station. The mother bent her knees ready to jump... she glanced down at the infant huddled at her breast, then laid it on the platform as she fell underneath the approaching train.

The train screeched as the driver tried to stop but to no avail. She had been electrocuted and her limbs had been severed. As the baby screamed in its pink, soft blanket, a young girl approached the infant, picked it up and cradled her.

"Do you know this child?" a woman asked her. The baby stopped crying as the young woman put her small finger in its mouth so she could suckle. The baby's blanket was wrapped tightly around her; she was hot and flustered, trying to wriggle out.

"The police will be here in a minute, you need to report this child has been abandoned. You can't just take it."

The young woman remained silent unable to speak. She was horrified at the stranger's insinuation that she would just go off with a strange child. The infant looked content and sleepy as she continued to suckle.

Police assembled on the platform and ushered people away from the dead body and the heinous scene. The child opened her eyes as she blinkered away a stray tear, her eyes were a beautiful shade of green. The baby was warm, so the stranger loosened the blanket and hidden within, was a snake shaped brooch with sparkling, green diamond eyes.

Three years later.

Hampstead, London - September 1975

Simone sat regally at the head of her dining table. The room was large and airy; big Georgian windows overlooked the detached houses opposite her home on Frognal Way in London's salubrious NW3. Simone was downstairs having lunch with her dearest friend, Yasmin El-Khayed; Sheikh Montieff El-Kayed's beautiful wife. They sat like royalty as their lunch was carefully presented to them.

"Yasmin, how is your husband? I hope he is treating you well?"

"Of course." Yasmin smiled. "He indulges me and I enjoy being indulged. We have this in common." Both women smiled, they were so very happy with their good fortune to be married to such powerful men.

"And Richard? How is he?"

Simone lifted her arm to show the sparkling diamond bracelet around her wrist. "Yes, I am indulged. But sadly, I think my treats are as a result of his guilt. What can I do?" she tipped a morsel of cucumber into her mouth then chewed it slowly.

3

"Accept it. Like the rest of us. Our husbands come home to us, their dalliances and indiscretions are not our concern. Men do these things. They feel guilty, we forgive."

"Yes, I suppose they are rather lucky to have us don't you think?"

Yasmin nodded. "But let us not forget, that we too are lucky. The other women only temporarily borrow our husbands. We are secure and so are our children. It isn't complicated just a fact of life. How is Portia, your dear daughter?"

"Portia." Simone smiled and shrugged her shoulders as she thought about her adopted daughter. "My darling Portia. I adore her but she's rather headstrong. It bothers me sometimes. She can be difficult." Yasmin smiled at her. "May I offer you some sparkling Italian water or perhaps some champagne? I'm exhausted from the day."

"I think that perhaps water would be better my dear. I don't drink alcohol."

Simone was highly embarrassed that she had forgotten. She blushed but Yasmin was kind, looked the other way and poured herself some water until Simone could compose herself. "Yes, of course. I'm so silly sometimes."

"Not at all. You're the perfect hostess and generous; you wanted to spoil me with your best champagne. An easy mistake."

Simone took the linen napkin off her lap and walked towards the windows which were dressed with white voile and luxurious, damask rose coloured velvet curtains. The room was stuffy from the wooden crates, straw and padding so she opened the window to allow in some fresh air.

They had recently had a large delivery of German porcelain from the family's factory near Cologne. As the grandson of Mighelli D'Allegro, Richard had inherited the family fortune and business; as its chairman, he had ensured their well-guarded reputation as one of the most expensive producers of unique, jewel embellished, porcelain sculptures. Nature scenes, beautiful women, animals, normally designed and made to a specific client request. Designed in Italy, made in Germany and with diamonds sourced from the world's finest diamond exchanges. For all sculptures commissioned by royalty, he would personally check before their international despatch. The last ornament had now been sent so the room could be reopened after full security measures had been adopted to keep the ornaments safe.

Simone was perturbed that her home was used as a 'post room'. It was inconvenient that she did not have absolute use of the house and with respect for her personal diary.

The view onto the road was onto one of the prettiest in Hampstead. Some of the houses had black iron, electric gates, some had brick walls. The roads were clean as the homeowners all had staff who strictly adhered to the street's rules with respect to aesthetics and presentation. Regularly trimmed hedges separated the properties rather than fences and each front was immaculate and well kept. Front gardens were generally paved so the car fleet could be displayed, with lesser cars or classics being stored in the garages.

After the Italian au pair, Sophia, had finished serving lunch, she presented coffee with some delicately prepared exotic fruit. Simone left the table and followed her outside.

"Where Mrs. Delaney the housekeeper?"

"I am no sure Mrs. D'Allegro. Her day off perhaps."

"Day off? Are you sure? But there's so much to do."

"If she not here, I sort out."

"And do YOU know what needs 'sorting' Sophia?"

"Cucina. The kitttt.. chen. The wood… wood floors" she continued.

"Then?" Simone continued.

"Piscina. The Pool."

"The swimming pool Sophia. Have somebody chlorinate the pool. I may have a swim later" she told her slowly to ensure Sophia understood.

"Si. I will."

Simone retreated back into the dining room. "Ah" she sighed. "A woman's work is never done. I really do need a holiday. It's a nightmare maintaining this house but Richard insists we need it. I would prefer a penthouse overlooking Hyde Park but what can I do? Richard is adamant." She shrugged her shoulders and had hoped for some sympathy. Yasmin smiled and didn't pass comment.

The staff were busy, so Portia and Celeste sat undisturbed in Simone's bedroom as they played with her make-up, clothes and jewellery. Above the headboard, was a large oil painting of Portia's mother, Simone; Richard had made this his personal project and commissioned a Royal Academy artist. Her blonde hair fell on her shoulders like endless golden ribbons and she wore a seductive black negligee which was so delicately arranged, the viewer felt that at any second, it might slip and reveal her naked body beneath. The artist had signed his name in thick, black paint as if a declaration of pride at his creation. An ostentatious, large gold frame completed the effect.

Portia took a long pearl necklace and put it around her neck; it reached her knees. She then picked up the brightest red lipstick she could find and tried to copy her mother's technique as she put it on her lips. She made a face as she pouted and stared at herself in the mirror. The bright red lipstick made her beautiful green eyes look even more stunning. She mimicked her mother as she adored herself in front of the mirror, then she scrambled into the large walk-in wardrobe. She pulled at the clothes, hoping some would fall down as she couldn't reach the clothes rail. A Christian Dior white ball gown tumbled down on top of her. Celeste pulled at it as both girls giggled. Portia wasn't sure how to get into the dress so lifted up one end and climbed into it, ripping the dress as she fell over whilst staining the silk with the red lipstick. She wiped it in attempt to try and hide the stain. A small mark turned into a largish blemish. Soiled rather than pristine, she tugged at some other clothes like a kitten scratching at furniture, she ruined everything she touched.

"Portia?" Celeste asked. "Does your mummy have shoes? My mummy has two pairs. One for work and one for when she goes out."

"Of course. My mummy has lots and lots of shoes. Silly Celly."

"I hate being called Celly. My name is Celeste."

"Well I like Celly. So I will call you Celly. Like I call my dolly Dolly. And that's that." She walked over towards the stacks of boxed designer shoes at the far end of the closet. She took out the bottom box which caused the balanced boxes on top to also fall down. Lids flew off at random and shoes spilled onto the carpet. Portia took out some black, high-heeled stiletto shoes from the pile whilst Celeste took out some red satin, cocktail sandals.

They had difficulty getting into the shoes and walking; Celeste tripped and the stiletto broke. As she fell over, she started to cry from the shock of her fall. Portia put her arm around her and hugged her. "Doesn't matter my little princess" she said, mimicking her mother's voice and tone. "They're my favourite shooos and I loved them... but it doesn't matter. I could never be too angry with youuuu."

Portia checked Celeste's foot and it seemed fine, so she stood up and walked over to her mother's dressing-table. She took out the make-up brushes which had been neatly lined up and a selection of cosmetics. Chanel, Dior, YSL, she applied blusher to her friend's face. They giggled and Celeste sneezed as some powder went up her nose.

"Let me find some green stuff for your eyes" Celeste said. "Because you got nice eyes like my dolly." She found some eye-shadow and a blusher brush and tried to apply. Portia looked like a clown and some eye make-up went into her eyes; it made her cry.

"Sorry Portia. The brush was too big for my littal hands."

Then they sprayed the perfume from a large crystal bottle. It was heavy and she dropped it. It broke into a thousand pieces. The room began to smell of perfume. They started to cough then giggling, they sat cross-legged on the floor as they spoke about nursery, their friends, teacher, the horrible Ms. Tathacote and the naughty little boys. Feeling uncomfortable they got up and crept onto the bed.

Portia was still wearing her mother's string of pearls, it caught on her arm and the string broke, releasing what felt like, thousands of pearl drops around the room. They scattered everywhere; under the bed, under the dressing table, across the carpet and into the pile of clothes.. "Will your mummy be angry, coz you broke her necklace?" Celeste asked.

"My mummy loves me" she said. So the girls carried on talking, then tired from their exertions, crawled under the duvet, laid their little painted faces onto the 1000 thread Egyptian cotton sheets and enjoyed a little nap before afternoon tea. Mrs. Delaney had brought in some Angel Cake and they were very excited and had already agreed they would share the pink layer.

Sophia screamed when she found the mess, the girls woke up and both started crying uncontrollably. They were frightened and didn't know what was wrong.

"Celeste, Portia, please, please be quiet," she begged. "Your mother will kill you both." This last comment made them cry even more. Why would Portia's mother kill them? Both girls ran out of the bedroom and downstairs.

"Mummy," Portia cried. "Sophia said you are going to kill us."

"Why? What have you done?" she yelled.

Simone raced up the stairs and was hysterical when she saw the bedroom. Portia was smacked until her legs stung and red from the assault. All cakes, sweets and chocolates were banned from the house. All party invitations were to be declined, friends were not allowed to visit and especially Celeste. Simone screamed repeatedly: "How could you? How could you? You hateful children. Portia... You hateful and spiteful child. My precious, precious things. You have killed me with what YOU HAVE DONE."

Celeste cried and started jumping up and down in fear, trying to block out the pain of what was happening. Portia was also crying and also started to jump up and down.

"Stop it. Stop it. You naughty, naughty girls" Simone screamed. "You've ruined everything. All my lovely things. MY THINGS...." Portia tried to hug her but Simone pushed her away and outside of the bedroom onto the upstairs landing.

"Is this how you behave where you're from?" Simone shouted at Celeste.

Celeste tripped and accidentally pushed Portia over who had already started to go down the stairs in an attempt to run away from the trauma and upset. Portia tumbled and started to fall down a few marble stairs of the winding staircase. Celeste immediately lent over and grabbed her dress. A hushed silence as Simone and Sophia gasped in horror.

"Don't worry Portia. I'm here." Calm and collected whilst the onlookers stood frozen, frightened by the near accident which had just been averted by a controlled Celeste. "Take my hand" she said. Her little voice, choked with fear for her friend's safety but also mature and positively reactive. Celeste was assured by Portia's confidence. They held hands tightly and were frightened to move.

"Please don't let go Celly. You're my bestest friend."

Simone stepped down and carried both girls to the top of the stairs. Too shocked and stunned to reprimand further, the thought of what potentially could have happened frightened her. So very easily, it could have been even worse which was almost impossible.

That was the only time in their entire lives, that Celeste and Portia did not see each other for a week. Separated from each other, both girls cried every day, there was an emptiness that would haunt them forever. Celeste called her favourite doll Portia and pretended her friend was with her at all times. Portia would not be separated from her little white rabbit. Both girls barely spoke and seemed to be traumatized from their enforced separation.

Upon their reunion they promised never to play Pretend Princesses again and a lock was put on the parents' bedroom doors. Celeste's parents were relieved that it hadn't happened to them but sympathized with Simone's plight and absolute distress.

Portia had to be very quiet, because her mother slept a lot over the next few weeks; her father took some time off work and her grandmother came to stay with them. It was a lovely week having her parents and grandmother around but she was aware there were less cuddles and less excitement about her drawings.

"You're a naughty girl" her grandmother would reprimand. But Portia didn't understand. She was only doing what her mother did every day. Except when you're a little girl, it's a bit harder because everything was too big. She needed more practice and would wait until she got taller and bigger before trying on the clothes and shoes again. Perhaps there would be less mess when they fitted properly.

Many shopping trips later, plus deliveries and parcels, everything went back to normal and Portia was the princess again. And next time, if her and Celeste would be separated, they made a pact to hide in the garden. They agreed that if their parents thought their children were missing, they would be more concerned about that than being horrible. This was their pledge and they swore to honour it until they died.

London, England
May 2005

"Celly, I absolutely love this one" Portia told Celeste as they looked at a multi-million pound mansion in an estate agent's window. "Just perfect for me." The specification read more like a Cluedo board than a residential home. Portia was excited; her imagination was ignited with ideas for decorations, furniture and colours. Plus she knew her father would commission the best sculpture ever as a new home gift. A testament of love for his daughter.

"You're so material Portia. And how are you going to get it?" Celeste asked. "Certainly NOT through YOUR hard work. You don't work. Daddy pays all your bills whilst you pretend to be stressing over a great curriculum vitae and interviews. You flunked school, you flunked college and in case anything has been missed, you have flunked everything else. You are a serial flunker and have the attention span of a…. a gnat!"

Portia shrugged: "So what…" she said flippantly but her tone could not mask the inherent sadness. "Not everybody can be happy as a primary school teacher… like you."

"Stop feeling sorry for yourself," Celeste rebuked. "You are beautiful and loved by your parents."

She shrugged again: "Still not the same blood. Anyway, daddy's not stupid. He knows I'm not a career girl. Probably thinks I might have been more successful if his REAL daughter."

"So you're adopted. No parents could have loved you anymore than your two. They couldn't have their own child – so invested all their time and love into you. You're quite an ungrateful brat – despite being my best friend."

"I can't explain it Celly. It's like your part of something but also an outsider. Your closest family, your parents are unknown. It leaves a void, a big empty gap which could explain so much; even basics like do I look like them? Is there some hereditary disease I should know about? So many questions and no answers, just a big empty hole. They can love me but I can't help craving the woman who gave birth to me – to ask her why? Why did she leave me? Who was my father? I know my parents adore me but still inside, I feel abandoned."

"But you can't ask her you know she's dead. And just because you've been adopted doesn't mean you have the next best option. Perhaps what your parents have given you in the way of love, support and security are far more than your real mother was capable. Have you ever considered that?"

"Or so they say. What proof do I have of anything? It doesn't help. So this poses more questions. Why? Why jump in front of a train when you had a two week old baby? Wasn't I worth living for? Did she want to jump with me? Would I be better off dead? Is this true? It doesn't make sense. Nothing makes sense. Me being alive doesn't make sense."

"Stop it. Stop it. Honestly – you'll drive yourself nuts and me too. You'll never know. Accept it. Move on. You're loved, does it matter Simone's not your birth mother. Your birth mother couldn't look after you and another couple took responsibility."

"But you can't stop wondering. You don't know what's nature or what's nurture. There's this incessant conflict – the endless questions that will never be answered. Nobody can answer them. Was my mother a prostitute who was down on her luck? Some tart that didn't even know who my father was. Or was she protecting a married man who abandoned her? Who? What? Why? When? She had no identification; nobody knew her name, who she was? Where she was from… Nothing."

"You're loved by your parents. For starters they had no obligation to you – loved you because you were a baby destined for the Social Services route. They took you in, gave you everything, including love, security and wealth; they never asked for anything in return. Their love was unconditional. Agreed Simone is sometimes hard work but don't you ever ask yourself, what you actually gave back?" She paused to give Portia a moment to consider her point. "Your life could have been very different. At least, you should be grateful. You could have been adopted by paupers, then what? You certainly wouldn't be planning a life of luxury and looking at mansions."

"You make sense Celly but I can't help it."

"The girl can't help it." Celeste sighed and shook her head. "Portia, life's not a fairy tale. At some point, you will have to face reality."

"As for grateful?" Portia laughed. "They chose me not the other way around."

"You have the brooch. You have something from your birth mother."

"I have my life" she replied tartly. "But it hardly makes up for a lifetime's void. If my mother really was down on her luck and opting to commit suicide rather than take responsibility for me, why didn't she pawn that brooch?"

"You mean the one attached to your blanket when she jumped?"

"Yes. Simone wanted a doll. A fashion accessory that she could dress. I don't get the brooch and its purpose. Only that it's my connection with what I really am. And it's precious. I rarely see it. My father keeps it in the safe."

"I was there when you were growing up Portia. You are wrong. Simone takes herself very seriously but with whatever love is left after her own self-love, *(they laughed)* she loves YOU. You had everything…including love. You need to accept yourself Portia and if you need counselling, go for it. But there are times when you are unbearable in your incessant need for attention and affection. You make people think you love them, but you don't. It's all a game. A sad game. But you're the loser because actually, you have everything." She paused. "Did you ever find out what that brooch was all about?"

"No. But that's why we're here and going to that exhibition: Bejewelled Animals with Diamonds. In my spare time I try to research."

"Research?" Celeste laughed. "By going to an exhibition in Hampstead. That's really hard work."

"So what. However it should have been a tiger not a snake! I hate snakes. Not sure if I should be impressed or insulted."

"You're too cynical Portia. We're talking about your life and parents, but really, the main problem is the only man you ever really loved, James. He loved you and like everyone else, you broke his heart with your cynicism and a rather distasteful trait of being unable to forgive anybody for anything. Goes way back with you."

"Perhaps" she shrugged. "Does it really matter? He was a big boy. I am sure it didn't take too long to replace me in his affections."

"Portia" Celeste retorted. "You are materialistic, selfish and probably not entirely capable of love. You probably love yourself, just a bit too much. And in some respect are relatively deluded. Perhaps you're Simone's love child and she's only adopted you to cover up a secret affair?"

"My mother – an affair? I'm sure she just about tolerates my father but another man? Hilarious. As for love, I loved James. Until he went off with that slutty waitress. A waitress? So common." Celeste hugged her and hoped that Portia might just crawl out of her shell-like chrysalis in order to shed her vulnerability despite the fake bravado.

"I loved James and really thought he was The One. I couldn't bear to be hurt like that again."

"He was hurt too Portia. You were perfect for each other."

"No, because at the first opportunity he betrayed me."

"Then you betrayed him. He had a moment's madness. He begged you for forgiveness. He was drunk and so what she was a waitress. She has feelings too. She got pregnant."

"Her fault."

"Takes two Portia. Plus two or rather three wrongs don't make a right and all that…"

"Look it's history now. Why bring up? Why analyse? I've moved on and so has James. He's been living with Caroline for six months now and rumour has it he will probably marry her."

"But would drop her in an instant if he had a chance again with you. James was far too deep for just sex. He was a good man. He slipped up. He's always asking about you, always concerned. Trying to find a way to get back into your life. He pleaded with you for eight months. You stop people loving you; you make them suffer as if they have to prove their worth. You make them love you, only to drop them at a whim. You enjoy inflicting pain."

"No I don't. I have feelings too…"

"Yeah. Right! Only a real friend can be as blunt as this, so don't be angry. I'll always be there for you but sometimes you need to hear the truth. You go off at a tangent and without accountability could end up harmful to others as well as yourself."

"Let's stop this. James is history. Also he never got that expat job in Dubai. He could never have supported me properly. I have no illusions… You know what I want, have been telling you since I was at nursery. You can't accuse me of being fickle; I've never swayed from my ideal."

"And your point?"

"Let's get a coffee Celly? I'm tired."

Celeste had always hoped that at some point, there may have been just a semblance of hope that Portia's sexuality and stubborn personality would mellow but it was no use. As for Portia's motivation to marry for money…. Well that was Portia. She couldn't risk financial struggle.

They walked away from the estate agent's shop and in silence. Walking down Hampstead High Street in London, their step was slow and thoughtful as they approached the gallery.

"Oh blast! It's shut" Portia exclaimed.

"We shouldn't have been distracted and chatted."

"Come back tomorrow?" Portia asked.

"Sure. Let's have a coffee and think about what to do next."

Despite their differences, both hoped they would always stay friends. To be part of each other's lives, share the good times, the difficult times and even their children. They saw an empty table and sat down. A waiter approached and passed them two large menus.

Two handsome men were seated at the next table. Portia caught their gaze and started to smile and flirt. Tears forgotten and James irrelevant, Portia wanted to play with her new audience.

"Stop it Portia," Celeste whispered from behind the menu.

"Why?"

The taller man of the two lent over and asked if he could join them. Portia smiled then glanced down at a vacant chair. "I'm sure I've seen you before" he said to Portia. "Were you at the exhibition?"

Celeste cringed, looked at his friend and raised her eyebrows. "Boring!" she said, loud enough for everybody to hear.

"I'm not boring. My name is Max. Max Schultzmann to be precise" the taller man replied, looking to Portia for back-up. "Do you think I'm boring?"

"That depends doesn't it," she said. "Depends on what Max does for a living. And no, we weren't at the exhibition, we might be coming back tomorrow. We just missed it."

"That's a shame. Today was the last day. Did I hear your friend called you Portia? Very nice name. Unusual."

"But… And yes, I am Portia."

"It was only on for three days. Not much demand. And a private collector has purchased most of the pieces. I heard he was a Russian recluse. Even I can't trace him and I'm very well connected… Sorry my darling."

Max noticed her disappointment. "You're very beautiful." He stroked her hand.

"See Celly, I am a romantic." Portia teased.

"Are you?" Max asked. "I'm a romantic. A very passionate one."

A waitress approached their table, Portia asked for an espresso and one for Celeste too in case the latter was tempted to leave. Max ordered a beer for him and his friend. They whispered something in French.

"My French is rather schoolgirl but I do speak Italian."

"That's a shame. Beautiful, sexy language. But do you speak the language of love?" Portia didn't reply.

"So how many languages do you speak?"

"Well there's English, French and German. All fluent... You're beautiful Portia" he repeated, wondering whether she would respond to the flattery.

"I'm told that all the time" Portia replied then purposely yawned. "Can't you be a bit more original that that? Even if you can ask me in three, whoops I mean FOUR languages. But sadly not Italian... I know what interests me and by the way, I do have an agenda." she teased. "Do you?" There was an awkward silence. "Where do you work?"

"In London. An account manager for a large advertising agency. But that's not the basis for my wealth. Trust funds. Much easier to be given it than to work."

Portia looked over at Celeste and smiled. "Gift from heaven" she mouthed. She took a beautiful enamel pen from her handbag, handed him a piece of paper and the pen; he wrote down his business, mobile and home phone numbers.

"I'll call you" she said as she took the paper. "But it won't be immediately – when I'm ready."

"And so I'll wait..." he replied. "I'm sure you're worth waiting for." His light blue eyes had a glimmer of lustful desire. Soft blonde hair which had been flicked back; he was fashionable and impressive. Everything Portia liked.

"If it gets any more banal, I'll throw up" Celeste said in monotone.

"I'm in advertising too" his friend said with a French accent, hoping to replicate the same success as Max.

"And I'm not looking for a marketer" Celeste replied. "So looks like you're on a 50% success rate. Mr. Frenchman – you lost."

"My name is Andre" he said indignantly.

"And I'm sorry Andre. I'm looking for love not money." Portia frowned at her. Sometimes Celeste was just too embarrassing.

A week later and Portia had been relentless. "Oh come on Celly. Please. It won't be fun without you and Andre was really taken."

"Portia please get real. You practically gave Max the green light for sex and you expect me to tag or shag along."

"No. I was just being my normal, happy, flirty self. I couldn't help it. He really is handsome and just so perfect. He's good-looking, charming, potential great future and more importantly, adores me!"

"He's on a promise Portia. You came on too strong."

"So maybe slightly more flirty than normal. But he wants to see me again, I want to see him too but it would be so much more fun if you doubled-up with Andre. Anyway, you weren't that friendly to him and he's still keen on you. Not used to women being so dismissive, he respects you… And you've got to admit, he is extremely handsome, probably even more than Max and with that incredible sexy, French accent."

Portia had an annoying habit of always ensuring that she got her own way. Celeste thought about Andre. She had noticed his good looks but his excessive confidence turned her off. Maybe she had judged him too quickly.

"We're just talking dinner and Max said if you came too, we could go anyway we wanted. I was going to suggest we fly to Paris. Is that a bit much for a first date? Sure we'll be spoilt and indulged and we haven't promised anything. What's wrong with dinner? We do that all the time, Come on Celly. For me. You know I'd do it for you. What's there to lose?"

Back home in her parents' small flat above a William Hill bookmakers shop, Celeste thought about Portia. So certain of her future, so animated in her excitement of things to come. She always got exactly what she wanted. Portia attracted men like bees to flowers. If only she felt even one-tenth of Portia's confidence but she didn't. Their friendship was close despite their different backgrounds.

Portia was beautiful, that was beyond doubt. With a daily beauty routine and attention to her physique, which had ensured an ideal weight and proportions for fashion and male fantasy.

Celeste was different. Despite living quite near Hampstead, her address was geographically more Cricklewood. Her family were working class and as the only child, her parents had indulged her with a private school education so she might have the opportunity to enrich her life and with a better future than they had enjoyed. Their lifestyle and home suffered as a result of the fees.

Looking at her mobile, Celeste now had ten texts from Portia. "Please?"

Her pleas and desperation was fast becoming unbearable. "For me…"

Then *ding* and another text.

Angrily Celeste picked up the phone. "Only if you'll STOP ASKING. At this point, if you didn't know them already, I'd tell you ALL my secrets just to stop your texts and nags."

"Come on, don't be like this. It'll be fun and if not, we'll ditch them and go out afterwards without them."

"OK OK. But not on a school night, it's coming up to exam time and I'm in at 7 a.m. every morning to make sure the pupils are focussed. Only if it's Saturday. Assuming they're not busy with other women…"

"I'll sort it out. Leave it to me. Max and Andre will be so pleased. So assume this Saturday."

"I await your call Portia. But no other day. Only Saturday. And I mean it. I have responsibilities."

An hour later Portia texted Celeste to say, they would be dropping into a Belgravia gallery at 6 p.m. for a private viewing of a diamond sale. Dinner was booked for 7 p.m. at Trader Vics, Park Lane Hilton.

Portia wore a sexy red, Givenchy low cut dress and long, gold rope necklace with matching earrings. A complementary small red Prada bag, Christian Dior shoes and a Rolex watch, which had been purchased specifically for that evening. Celeste wore a plain black dress and pearls, very much in the style of Coco Chanel.

Standing outside of the gallery behind Harrods, Max and Andre appeared looking equally dashing. Max wore an Armani suit and fashionable, Italian leather shoes, Andre's suit fitted perfectly and had clearly been designed and cut for him.

"You both look beautiful" Max exclaimed. "You're looking delightful – almost too good to eat" he proclaimed as he took Portia's hand. She giggled at the sexual undertones. Celeste frowned. "But first, I need to sort out some business. There was a piece at that exhibition that rather took my eye. I want it and I GET – what I want." Portia raised her eyebrows then smiled.

"But hopefully it isn't always too easy for you."

"It generally is."

They entered the gallery and Max immediately noticed some Oscar Heyman and Ulrich Lehr pieces. He stared at a beautiful flower made of precious jewels; his face went red and he started to wave his arms around whilst demanding to see the owner. Max insisted the piece was a fake. He was unnecessarily offensive. The owner shrugged off his protestations and attempted to walk away but

Max's behaviour was irrational and professionally insulting. People in the shop began to leave, uncomfortable with the almost frightening and unacceptable display of bad behaviour.

"You're a fraud" he shouted. "You're selling fakes. You should be ashamed. This isn't a genuine Lehr" he shouted, pointing his finger at the owner's eyes. His mood swing alarmed Celeste. "You're a fraud" he kept shouting at the owner.

A young man in his mid-twenties who had been standing quietly in the corner, observing the scene stepped forward and intervened. "I'm sure there's some mistake" he said gently. "I've known Mr. Kauff for many years. His information and guarantees have stood up and not once, have any of his pieces been disputed. Plus I am here to purchase a particular piece from the exhibition myself."

"And just who are you? They were sold to a Russian."

"Firstly, my name is Jean-Pierre Hughes. And like you, I'm an interested party for diamond brooches of the 20s and 30s. Not everything was sold. Mr. Kauff had a prior arrangement that was honoured by the gallery. I also buy beautiful things. All the pieces have been authenticated – I assure you, they are genuine."

"And how would you know?" Max demanded. He had little patience for people he didn't like and didn't bother to conceal his contempt. He felt as if his body would explode from the anger within.

Jean-Pierre continued: "I am very familiar with a specific type of diamond jewellery. Especially pieces designed in the 1920s and I regularly consult with Mr. Kauff and if I'm in doubt about a specific item, I trust to his judgement and discretion. Mr. Kauff is an internationally recognised authority, I would suggest you show him some respect" and he nodded towards the shop's owner. "I assure you." He spoke with authority, calmly, and with an air of dignity that made resistance difficult. His English was perfect but his accent was European. He was confident and self-assured.

Max's mood began to mellow. "Let us be a little calmer… you have beautiful friends, why spoil your evening?"

His eyes were deep and sensual, enticing like a swimming pool of erotic pleasure and Celeste felt herself drowning.

Then Jean-Pierre saw Portia and for a moment, the world seemed to stop. As he looked at her beautiful face, he felt moved; she took hold of his desires in a way that no other woman had ever touched him before. When she smiled back, pleasant and uncomfortable as her boyfriend was closely watching her, he felt regret that she had sold herself too cheap. She was worth more than her male friend. He was both attracted and simultaneously repulsed. Something about her make-up, the strong perfume, the overt sexuality… it angered him. Reminded him of something… Or somebody.

Jean-Pierre smiled, turned around and from behind his back, slipped his card into Celeste's jacket pocket. He had to find a way to see the other woman again but not in front of her boyfriend. Perhaps her friend would help him.

Celeste felt the card slip into her pocket but didn't bring attention to it. When he looked at her again, she just nodded. She felt a spark, something powerful that linked her to him. More than his gaze, the way he held himself, so proud and upright. He had dignity, confidence and a secret magnetic power which made him irresistible. She imagined him naked then felt slightly ashamed of the thought. She blushed but didn't want to let go of this image. She looked at his trousers, they weren't tight but when he moved, she saw the outline of his legs beneath the material.

When he looked around for one last glimpse at the group of friends, he was looking for Portia. And Celeste was looking at him.

Max stormed out of the shop and slammed the door behind him. He was oblivious to the fact that Portia, Celeste and Andre were still there.

"You must excuse my friend" Portia said on his behalf, feeling compelled to protect him. "I think he's having a bad day! Sorry!" She shrugged her shoulders. Mr. Kauff shook his head with disgust. "I'm sorry." Mr. Kauff stared at her but said nothing.

They all left the gallery and the shop was closed. Portia and Celeste walked on ahead. Portia opened her bag and took out her snake brooch. She had hoped that perhaps there might have been some time to ask about her piece. Celeste looked at it too. "Every time you try and pursue this Portia, something goes wrong. The gallery is shut and then an argument which makes it impossible to discuss. Perhaps it's fate telling you to just leave history where it is – in the past."

"Perhaps." She clenched her hand around the brooch. "But will I ever know?"

"When the time is right. And now is not that time. If ever is the right time."

Max and Andre stood for a few minutes in the street and argued. Andre tried to calm Max's mood and kept pointing towards Portia and Celeste. Max punched the air in anger. Andre grabbed his shoulders and for a moment, it looked as if the two men would fight. Raising both hands with palms facing Andre, his gesture was one of suppressed anger, then calm as his movements and body language showed acceptance; as if he had heard the words and had agreed with the message. The rabid dog had calmed. Tranquilized by some meaningful point which took the venom out of his emotion and the bite out of his bark.

As the two couples walked into the hotel lobby, heads turned, men whispered, women were envious. The women stole the show within just a few minutes of their arrival. Were the women with dates? Or were they professionals who had just picked up some evening trade? They turned left and walked downstairs into the restaurant.

Trader Vics was like an exotic Polynesian beach venue. Max had clearly tipped the sommelier (probably in excess) as a bottle of chilled Bollinger appeared and was promptly poured in all their glasses. "Good evening Mr. Schultzmann. I hope you have a pleasant evening."

"Let our evening flow with Bollinger and your delicious cocktails" he declared as he flamboyantly gave the waiter a large wad of notes. Portia seemed to flow with his moods but Celeste was alarmed. She also couldn't forget the stranger in the shop. She wanted to take his card out of her pocket and peek at his name. She wondered if the card would still be warm from his touch.

Portia was animated in her excitement about the evening.

"Another Scorpion Bowl for my friends here and for this beautiful lady, a Trader Vics Passion Cocktail." He touched Portia's leg. His hand moved up her leg and towards her thigh. She didn't stop him. He wondered how far he could go…

Within a few minutes, another round of cocktails appears. Celeste knew that Max was a man who should not be crossed. Max frightened her; the stranger, Jean-Pierre intrigued her.

The waiter approached the table and cleared the plates. "Some dessert?" he offered.

"I think that perhaps, I would like you to be dessert Portia…"

"I'm sure whatever's here, will taste better… than me!" she whispered.

"You bad, bad, naughty girl. Just what I like. Just what I need. Am sure you are delicious…"

The waiter still hovered. Celeste ordered some coffee for Portia. Out of politeness Andre had one too.

The more Portia drank, the lower her dress sunk. Her laughter and pouring over Max was uncomfortable for Andre and

Celeste who were at first base with respect to elementary conversations with a stranger.

Max's flirtations and intentions were embarrassingly obvious. Andre tried to put his arm around Celeste but she stared at him as if to say *you just dare!* He didn't and their conversation remained polite. Three bottles later, Max and Portia were virtually kissing. Celeste was disgusted. "Portia – pull yourself together. You look like you'd have sex on the table."

"Ssshh" Portia replied. "What's wrong with you – I'm simply having a good time. Silly Celly."

"You look like a good time. I think it's time we went home. Get ready with your good-byes and see you soon."

"You go if you want to – I'm not."

"Hey girls – let's continue the party back at my flat."

"Yes let's" Portia piped up.

"Let's NOT," Celeste interrupted. Sliding her hand into her jacket pocket, she checked again that the card was still secure. It was. Despite Portia's protestations and clear need for protection, Celeste couldn't stop thinking about the stranger and resented being with Portia, Max and Andre when perhaps she could have been speaking to him. However her loyalty to Portia was ultimately more important. Portia couldn't be trusted.

"She's had far too much to drink and I think it's time I took her home. Thanks for a great evening but I need to take this little, drunk lady, home before she says or does anything she'd regret... Portia. I'm going to the powder room. Why don't you join me?"

"Whoops. Can tell the teacher's angry. Sorry miss," she slurred and giggled. "I'm in biggggg trouble" and she giggled again. Standing up her stance wasn't steady so Max supported her.

"I've got a little present for you," he teased her. "But I forgot to bring it with me this evening…"

"I like presents" she cooed back. Her eyes sparkling with delight.

"Why don't we all go back to my flat for an innocent, drinks only, post-dinner cocktail?"

"No thank you. And that's on behalf of me and Portia," Celeste stated flatly. "I think we're all up to our eyeballs in cocktail and Scorpions."

"I want to go. I want my pressie." Portia sounded like a spoilt child about to have a tantrum. As if there was ANYTHING, she didn't have.

"Please Portia. You're embarrassing, like a stupid child. I'd expect more from my kindergarten crowd than this. You've a jewellery box full of gems, why this? Have you no shame? I want to leave. And I want to leave NOW."

"You can't tell me what to do. You're not the teacher now. I can make my own decisions and I want my present. And I really want….. YOU" she said pointing to Max. He smiled like a hunter who had just killed a wild beast. Albeit this animal was trapped by her desires, greed and insatiable materialistic appetite.

"I can't leave you like this. Oh Portia, why do you do this? Andre, please, don't tell me you're part of this?"

Andre was not impressed with Max's behaviour. Whatever was going to happen next, it was clear that Andre had not been part of any plan.

"Max, come on. Let her go 'ome with her friend. We will go out. Find a club or someplace else. We can have fun without them. It 'az been a good evening. Leave it at zat."

Portia giggled and Max cuddled her in order to support. Andre took Celeste to one side. "I'm sorry Celeste. Zis is not nice. I am not part of it and I feel a little ashamed of Max. He iz my friend. We do not do this, get girls drunk then take back to a flat. It iz not elegant. I promise you, I had no part in thiz." He raised his eyebrows.

"If you have a shred of decency, tell Max to let her go and I'll get us a cab home." He nodded.

"Max, come on, the girl iz drunk. Let her go home with 'er friend."

"But I don't want to go home" Portia argued. "And I feel tired and sleepy. If you don't want to come back Celly, then it's just a cosy me and Max. That rhymed. Me and Max... At Max's Flat. Me and Max. Max Me Max..." She giggled and Max laughed too.

"As well as being absolutely adorable Portia, you're also very funny. Perfect for me," Max teased her as he stroked her cheek. Portia's mascara had begun to run and it was making her eyes bloodshot.

"What do you want Celeste?" Andre asked her.

"Look Mrs. Worried Pops" Portia slurred. "We'll go back for just one drink, just one titsy littsy weeny drink. Then I promise we'll leave. We'll go together, I promise. Scout's Honour. Guide's Honour. Any Honour you want... Except my honour. Whoops!"

So the four of them got a cab and in silence, back to Max's flat in St. John's Wood. The journey was as embarrassing as the restaurant. As soon as they got in the cab, Max and Portia started kissing. He was touching her breast and thigh and despite her meagre protestations, her removal of his hand from her bosom was more of a show for Celeste and Andre who sat in silence. Celeste wondered if Max's display was a show for them. As if he wanted them to be watching him. Touching her, kissing her, sexually exciting her as she began to gasp and pant slightly.

"Do you like watching Celeste?" Max asked her. Celeste ignored him and looked out of the taxi window. "Am sure she puts on quite a show."

"You're a pig – we should have just gone home."

"No Celeste. We shouldn't. And Max, you're a very naughty boy. Very naughty boy. No more touching or flirting in front of Celly."

"I'm just trying to involve her. She looks lonely and sad. And Andre has let the side down."

"Sad. I'm bloody fuming. I didn't want to come out. Didn't want to be here. If possible I'm more disgusted with Portia than you. She's my friend. You're just disgusting. Beneath contempt."

"Talk dirty Celeste," Max teased. "I like it."

Max bent over and whispered in Celeste's ear: "Care to join us later? If Andre isn't interested, I could do you both…" Celeste went to hit him but Andre stopped her.

"Stop the cab" Celeste called out. "Stop the cab." The taxi pulled over to the kerb and Celeste lent over towards the door whilst simultaneously grabbing Portia. "Come on Portia. You'll regret this in the morning."

"I won't regret anything. We're just picking up my pressie and one little drink. If Max and I are having a little fun now, it's nothing. Just a little kiss…"

"Yes, just a little kiss" Max repeated. "Just a little…. Kissssss".

"Portia. I'm sorry but I can't be part of this. It's me or Max."

Portia looked at them both. "Don't be angry Celly. Just having some fun."

Max put his arm around her and stroked her shoulder. "It's from Tiffany. I would hate to give it to somebody else. I can't stop thinking about you and think you're very special…"

Portia defied Celeste and looked unwilling to budge. Celeste was faced with a dilemma, did she leave the taxi – or should she stay with Portia for however long and whilst whatever happened – happened? She was disgusted with her, this slutty looking tart who was selling herself to the devil. In that instant, the relationship changed and Celeste knew that despite the years, Portia would throw it up for a drunken ache between her thighs and the promise of something. But she couldn't leave her.

Celeste sat back in her seat and checked again that despite the exertions, the card was still in her pocket. It was.

"Drive on" Max called triumphantly. "Straight to St. John's Wood. There'll be no further stops. And I'll double your fare if you put your foot down. We're in a hurry."

Portia was sick in the bathroom, the experience helped to sober her up. She had a strong coffee and a headache. But a headache never stopped a sex kitten like Portia. If she had been drunk, Celeste would have dragged her out of the flat but she wasn't. She was sober enough to make her own decisions and she was adamant. She was going to have sex with Max which would not be difficult. He clearly had the same intention. They were both as hot as tom cats.

Max had bought her a gold love-heart. She loved it and showed her gratitude. They went straight into the bedroom and from the loud love-making moans and groans that could be heard outside, they were hard at it. For half an hour, orgasms, thrashing, squeaky bed springs, some slapping and ripping of clothes could be heard. When Portia screamed: "Fuck me harder" Andre turned up the volume on the television whilst trying to drown them out with a Poirot drama on television. The evening was a farce, the solemn old world of Agatha Christie as compared to an uninhibited modern world in the bedroom.

Andre and Celeste watched it in silence, oblivious to the story line or acting; just wanting the fiasco in the bedroom to end. When they'd finished, Portia almost fell out of the bedroom with a satisfied grin. Max appeared behind her wearing just a towel. He looked at Celeste and rubbed his hands. Behind Portia's back he mouthed, "Your turn."

Celeste called a cab and took Portia home.

Celeste hated Max; she never wanted to see him again and never forgave him for that first night. She never saw Andre again either. However, this wasn't a one-night stand, Portia and Max were inseparable from that first drunken and lustful night; Portia would not hear one word against Max. Sometimes it went against Portia that she was so loyal; even to a love rat. If Celeste dared to question whether he could be trusted, they would argue. Celeste never told Portia what Max had said to her – there was no point. She would not have believed it as his word against hers. When Portia fell in love, it was absolutely. But just as quickly, she could fall out again and Celeste hoped this would be a transitory fling.

Chapter 2

A year later Celeste's parents were killed in a car crash. Celeste was in shock. She just sat there as friends and family brought food and tried to comfort her.

Portia tried to comfort too but Celeste was too immersed in her grief to have any inclination to reconcile with Portia. Sitting there on her own, looking abandoned, confused and lost. Thinking about her parents, identifying their bodies, the protocol of death certificates and arranging the funerals. The burial. Tears. It felt surreal as if she wasn't really there. Knowing that when she went home – the flat would be empty. She would never smell her mother's cooking again. They had been over-protective, she wanted their protection now. With no brothers, sisters or cousins, an orphan without parents or extra family.

When her mobile rang and she saw Portia's number she didn't answer. They felt like strangers not friends since childhood. But then Portia turned up as she knew her calls were being ignored. "I'm so sorry Celeste" Portia said repeatedly. "I loved your parents too. They were very special." She rubbed Celeste's arm but the latter moved back. "Will we ever be friends again? I know you don't like Max but honestly he's fine. He's calmed down and we're very happy."

"I don't remember the last time you called me Celeste."

"I feel there's a distance. Celly was your pet name. I don't know how you feel about me now."

Celeste was quiet as she thought about their history, their lives, entwined. Could a man drive a wedge between their friendship? "I'm pleased you're happy Portia. I'm pleased everything is OK. And yes, you can still call me Celly."

"How are you?"

"How can I be?" She paused and tried to swallow her tears. Portia held her tight and then Celeste sobbed.

"Tell me Portia, tell me about you?"

"I'm with Max. And I know it wasn't the best of starts and I should have listened to you and maybe not been so headstrong but it wasn't just a one off. We're still together. I love him Celly. He's everything I ever wanted. He's everything I have ever needed. He's made me a better person. I need him. None of us know what's in store; I can't help but be impulsive about what I want."

"I know" Celeste said gently.

"If you get to know him – honestly, you'd like him too. Please, give him a chance?"

"Not now. My parents have just died. I need time to get used to my own situation, let alone yours."

As Celeste looked around the room, her parents lounge, their wedding photograph on the wall, photographs of her as a child with her parents standing either side of her, smiling her eyes welled with tears again. She wondered if she would ever run out of tears. Would she ever stop crying? Her pillars of support, now gone. Dead. Her mother's favourite Royal Doulton china in a cabinet. She remembered how carefully her mother would take out the china if she had guests over for tea or dinner. Her father's jacket still hung by the front door. Her mother's hats on the shelf above the coats. They would never be moved by them again. Only when she was ready to box them up.

There was a knock at the door. Mrs. Patel and Mrs. Ogabe from across the road popped in to see Celeste. They saw Portia sitting there and instinctively knew the women needed some space. Mrs. Patel went into the kitchen and saw that in the sink, crockery was piled high. Going to the china cabinet, she took out some cups and saucers: "Tea or coffee?" Celeste and Portia nodded and Mrs. Patel went back into the kitchen. As the kettle was boiling, she started to wash and clean-up the dirty dishes.

As Celeste was passed the tea she looked at it. Her mother was territorial about who touched her things. But her mother wasn't here to say no. And now she was drinking a cup of tea, from her mother's cup, when her mother would never have used her best china for a random drink. It would have been a special occasion. An important guest. And now, they were being used because there were no other cups.

"Celly, take a few sips. You're probably thirsty" Portia said gently.

"Thank you," she replied politely. But she had no intention of drinking it. Putting it on an empty chair next to her, she felt alone. Her parents had no family, she was an only child. She sat alone. She felt alone. She had nothing. Nobody. How could anybody understand how she felt?

Looking down at her shoes, she didn't want to look up. She wanted a tissue but didn't want to get up. She wiped her face on the torn blouse. Mrs. Ogabe walked into the room and passed her a tissue. Portia looked at her in a way which said *give us space.* So Mrs. Ogabe went back into the kitchen and helped Mrs. Patel.

She felt Portia take her hand. "I'm here Celly. I'll always be here for you."

"I know" Celeste whispered unable to speak.

Sitting in the chair, for a moment she felt as if her life needed to change. "Portia."

"Yes," she squeezed her hand. "I'm leaving here. I'm going to sell this flat and move away."

"You can't make a decision. Now is not the right time. You're not thinking straight. Come and stay with me at my parents for a little while until you can get yourself together."

"No Portia. My decision is made. Remember the man in the shop, the man that spoke to Max?"

Portia certainly remembered him. If she hadn't have been with Max, she may have given him her number. Portia paused as if needing to think: "Yes, vaguely... I just about remember him."

"We've been seeing each other and I've become rather fond of him. He's been very supportive. We only met a few times before the accident, he travels a lot but since then, he's been very kind. He's been very caring. I've become very fond of him, even though it's a bit quick."

"When have you been seeing him?" Portia asked, unable to disguise her jealousy.

"We've not spoken to each other Portia. There are things you don't know."

Portia nodded. Never before did Celeste have any secrets from her. She felt the relationship slipping away as Celeste spoke of this new love.

"I have nothing here, my parents are gone and living like this, is not the way forward for me. Jean-Pierre has asked me to go

41

to Paris with him whilst he's based there. He has a six month secondment but travels extensively with his work."

"When did it become serious?"

"I suppose the accident brought us close. Before that it was just as friends. He even asked about you and thought it might be nice for us all to meet up. Then the accident and things changed. I needed a friend. He was there and he cared. He is very kind."

"I see." Portia sat slightly back. So he remembered her. But now Celeste needed him and clearly, he preferred her.

"I want to get away. Get away from here."

"You're in shock, traumatised." Portia argued.

"I just know this is the right decision for me. I've lost my parents. I want to be with Jean-Pierre. I feel he is all I have."

"Will I see you before you leave?"

"Probably not."

"And if things don't work out with Jean-Pierre, don't you think you're maybe rushing things?"

"That's rather funny coming from you. I still remember that night. I don't remember you holding back... I'm sorry. I…"

"Touché. You're right. Not my best moment but we're still together."

"So at worst I'll come back. But there was chemistry between us the minute I saw him. It felt right. It never felt right before with anybody else."

"You're making big decisions but you're still grieving."

"No Portia. I don't want to trial this. I want to go to Paris with JP."

"JP?"

"Jean-Pierre."

"Yes, yes of course." Portia thought of him. In her position, she would probably have done the same. If anything, Celeste was becoming like her and it alarmed Portia. "I was just saying… When Celly? When are you going?"

"I have a lot of packing to do. Perhaps we will see each other before then but no promises. Let's just see."

"Is there anything I can do? Celly I know we've drifted but you'll always be my best friend. We've been friends forever. Nothing has separated us – even when we messed up my mother's wardrobe. Remember that?"

Celeste smiled. "I know Portia. But we're not children anymore. We've grown up and are too old to hide from the things we do. That part of our lives is now over and our pact has been honoured. Let's leave it there."

"I know" Portia said gently. "But it would be so nice to hear from you. From time to time."

"But without Max please."

"That's difficult for me to answer but if that's what you want, I'll try and come over. It's important you find some happiness. Life's not been too fair for you."

"What's fair? I'm just salvaging what I can."

"I'll always love you Celly. You've always been my dearest friend. Please don't block me out of your life."

"I won't" Celeste replied. But her tone was not convincing.

"Don't let Max come between us. A man can be replaced, a best friend can't."

"Please Portia," Celeste pleaded. "Let me go. You have your life; I'm entitled to have mine."

"So who will catch me when I fall?" Portia asked Celeste. There was a brief silence when they remembered the incident on the staircase when they were children.

In their hearts, they remembered the first time they were separated. The empty pain that had consumed them both. Maybe this time it would be different? Or at least it wouldn't gnaw.

T. E. Conway - Advertising Agency, London England

Max looked at the various straplines from the copywriters. A new and innovative approach to selling lipstick: **Lovely Lips for Loving Kisses.**

Underneath, a picture of a beautiful woman with a full pout wearing bright red lipstick. How trite. Would the target audience of women in their late teens/twenties buy the product based on that? He didn't know. At this moment in time, he didn't care either. At least he could look forward to Prague. He glanced at his email confirmation sitting in his Inbox. He was excited about their trip. Would he propose? They had been together for over a year now and she was trying very hard to move in. He smiled at her antics.   She had never worked and justified her time in order to look beautiful for him. He was aware of the serious dent in his finances since Portia joined the payroll but she was worth it.

She wasn't particularly well travelled and her elegance and sophistication was more about upbringing and an expensive Hampstead private school education, rather than by hands-on experience. Privileged and protected by doting wealthy parents, she was rather spoilt but very pretty and more importantly, in awe of him. She loved him and that would suffice. He loved women of which she was just one.

He stopped himself from thinking too much about her. No time now for unimportant thoughts. He picked up his cold Starbucks coffee and took a deep gulp. It was disgusting and actually made him even thirstier. He took out a bottle of still mineral water from his bag and drunk it from the bottle. Some drops dripped down the side and made a small mark on the desk. It annoyed him.

His phone rang: "….Hi Portia. Yes, received your email." He glanced down at his watch. He was busy and didn't have time to talk plus he wanted to check the confirmation. Was it accurate? Portia was lovely but could be aloof and often made silly mistakes. "…Yes, great… Really excited too… Yes, I saw it's had a multi-million pound refurbishment. We'll talk tonight. Dinner? Sure of course. Whatever you want… I really don't mind Portia. Whatever YOU want… Need to go…. Yes (he paused) … love you too..." He wanted the InterContinental or Sheraton, she wanted boutique and near to the Old Town Square.

He smiled in anticipation of their nights then opened the email and carefully read every detail. Pensively, he recalled a stag weekend he had shared with a few arty friends. He couldn't remember much but the credit card bill indicated a great and exorbitant trip! £1,426 in the hotel bar. £728 in a nightclub. He was pedantic about bills, invoices and noting exact amounts. A bottle of killer Czech absinthe, a drunken state which lasted three days then being stopped at Customs and subject to a painfully long interrogation. Portia thought these were a few days break with friends at stag parties; he didn't give her the details. She didn't need to know about the friends, alcohol or prostitutes.

He wiped the water stain off his desk with a Starbucks serviette. Then polished the area with a small piece of material he kept in his top drawer.

His favourite city was probably Vegas. As long as the clubs had beautiful women, the option of whores with an inclination and tolerance of a certain type of imaginative foreplay and fantasy, a certain amount of playful pain, alcohol and of course … his best friend Cocaine Charlie. *Work hard. Play hard.* Now he would be going to Prague for the shopping and to keep his 'girlfriend' happy.

For Portia, she liked Art Nouveau or boutique hotels. Their hotel the **Hotel Art Deco** was classic Portia. Max's grandfather had suggested it and as soon as she saw the details, she was animated in her excitement. Even before she read the description she knew this was what she wanted. But nobody's perfect – probably not even him! She really had to steer him to make the right decisions… for her.

Practically, it would not be difficult to transfer from Munich to Prague. He was looking forward to seeing his beloved grandfather who lived just outside of the city. He wanted to fly but she wanted to take the train. A six hour train ride but sadly he had no option. Portia said it would be romantic. She teased him and smiled so he relented but was annoyed. HE wanted to fly. Much more practical use of time than just sitting on a train. He sat on trains everyday getting into the City from his apartment in St. John's Wood. Married friends understood why he appeased her. Single friends teased him and said he was 'whipped'. But they all liked Portia. She was lovely and supposedly marriage material of a certain type… He didn't feel intimidated by her. Well perhaps a little! But that was all part of the upbringing and her mother's influence. A pretty little light blue, Tiffany box would always make her jump for joy. Yes, Portia would make HIS evenings delectable in Prague. And he wouldn't have to pay extra for the sex.

His phone rang and he was brought back to the here and NOW. All thoughts of Prague, Portia, trains and predatory, uninhibited Czech 'professional' women were instantly forgotten. It was the Loving Lips client and their demands for the campaign.

Looking at his inbox, thirty urgent emails had appeared. He looked over to the graduate sitting quietly in the corner. Always the first one to arrive to the office and always the last one to leave. He would even stay until 3 a.m. then back in the office by 7.30 a.m.

ready to start again. He was pale, clearly depressed, slumped over this computer and exhausted. Racking his brains for straplines, knee deep in research of clients' competitors, Nicholas did all the donkey work whilst he partied with the big guns.

"Nicholas," he called. "There's some urgent work to be done. I'm sending over some emails and as quick as you can. Whack out the replies and be ready for a meeting at," he paused knowing that he normally arrived at 7.30 a.m. "I think we better check-up at 7 a.m. tomorrow morning so you can give me the heads up. Make it a conference call rather than face-to-face. Got a big night with Lovely Lips." Max knew it would be a late night but as a senior executive, it gave him a certain feeling of self-indulgence bullying others. Nicholas was enthusiastic, a graduate who had probably worked all hours of the day and night to get the necessary grades to get into the agency. A member of the deluded masses who thought he would be entering a glamorous profession.

Nicholas wouldn't leave or complain. He was lucky to have a job. And 'he' Max enjoyed a certain self-gratification at harassing this young man who was trying so hard. Perhaps too hard; it was fun watching them lose that initial interest, observing their energy and enthusiasm slowly draining like a cat playing with a dying mouse until it was dead. Slow and tortuous, whilst using all the well-worn clichés and encouragement such as promises of promotion, the fantastic salary and bonus that would be theirs, if they could hold on throughout the demonic process which ascertained their strength, tenacity and determination to succeed in the back-stabbing, environment of the advertising world.

Looking back at the emails marked urgent, he saw Nicholas had requested a few days annual leave. *Nope* he thought then sent the reply: "Sorry mate, problems with coverage. Request denied." What would Nicholas do? Max smiled. Dare to do that and he would be the first out in the next headcount reshuffle. '*Put Up and Shut Up or lose your job'*. And if you 'dare' to complain, another agency wouldn't touch you. Small world. Everyone knows everyone. No secrets.

Returning his gaze and attention to the screens, he rolled up his sleeves and sitting on the edge of his seat, turned off his mobile phone, engaged with his three large screens, allowed himself a few more minutes whilst he pretended to read his emails whilst reminiscing a certain prostitute's expertise then emailed the Art Department: "Try Harder! Your designs are crap!!!!!!' As he pressed the send button, he felt his dick get hard.

Chapter 3

As Portia entered Waitrose in Finchley Road, north-west London, she contemplated a romantic dinner with Max. She wanted to treat Max to a specially prepared meal.

Excited about their forthcoming trip, she secretly hoped, it would be a turning point in their relationship. They loosely, lived together. She hadn't been invited to move in as such but she found ways to just always be needed. The concierge could receive parcels and other deliveries; however it was better if she received them. Max could be reassured, it would be put away and be safer. It took all her creative energies to find different ways to be important to him aside of course, the obvious, physical relationship.

He liked her cooking too. So tonight she would make something special. Looking at the delicacies, she picked up some foie gras, a small bottle of black truffles which would be finely sliced and to decorate a home-made dish of pasta. Aged parmesan and fresh herbs, creamy mushroom sauce… Buying the ingredients, she felt confident they would enjoy a wonderful evening together and of course, he would then want her to stay the night.

She saw a black taxi and extended her arm and starting waving. As he pulled up alongside her, she told him her destination: "St. John's Road, opposite Lord's Cricket Ground," then elegantly she climbed into the back, buckled up her seat-belt then clutched her expensive shop. Life was so wonderful after a little spending spree. She closed her eyes and sat back in the seat. She was so incredibly lucky. Everything was just so perfect.

She gave the concierge a familiar and friendly smile. He looked up and nodded and tried to recall who she was. "Madam?" he asked.

"Hi Philip. Visiting Mr. Schultzmann" she replied. "How is your wife? You mentioned she was in hospital."

"Yes, that's right" he said with surprise. "Sorry, I didn't realise I had said anything."

"You mentioned in passing. Last week you were clearly distracted and I asked what was wrong. So on my travels, I her picked some Godiva chocolates and a good book. She can keep herself amused until visiting time." Portia handed him the silver bag with the gifts inside.

Philip walked around to the front of the desk and kissed her on both cheeks. "I.. I don't know what to say?"

"Nothing. Just tell her that I wish her better."

"Of course. Thank you, thank you." He looked in the bag and smiled. "She will certainly enjoy the chocolates and the book is a very kind thought. It's Portia isn't it."

"Yes."

"You're very kind."

Portia blushed. "Not really, you mentioned it and I remembered. It's nothing. Honestly. I was just sorry to see you looking so sad."

"Hope you have a good day" he called.

She took the lift to the 3rd floor, no point getting hot and sweaty by walking, then carefully (so she wouldn't break her nails) took out Max's red and gold Chanel key chain from her red and gold, Chanel handbag; she let herself in and immediately opened the windows to get some fresh air into the apartment. Her mother was a firm believer in keeping rooms fresh. Perhaps she was turning into her mother? Rinsing her hands in the black and white, marble sink in the guest WC, she then moisturized her hands with some Harrods hand cream which was strategically placed next to the sink and on the polished, glass, gold edged shelf.

Looking around the apartment, she contemplated what was needed, then watered the plants, puffed up the pillows which were gently laid out on the black sateen duvet cover with matching sheets and pillow cases. She spruced up the room and linen with a few sprays of Jasmine air spray, then some more, short, sharp, squirts around the apartment. These few female touches certainly made his home far more cosy. Yes, she certainly made him happier she told herself assuredly.

As she was in the bedroom, she decided to put the spray back in one of his bottom drawers, rather than strategising a small space between his personal accessories and her tiny allocated area on his lower shelf. She wasn't giving up that miniscule space to a spray when she could put her moisturiser there!

Opening one of his bottom drawers next to the bed, she saw a photograph of them both. She was smiling and looked beautiful and happy. She smiled. Max looked quite stern. His light blue eyes and expression had a hint of boredom. As she went to replace the photograph, she noticed a brown envelope. Stamped on the front –

PRIVATE AND CONFIDENTIAL –

MAIL ORDER CATALOGUE –

TO BE OPENED BY ADDRESSEE ONLY.

She hesitated, it wasn't her business to look through his drawers however, he didn't need to know. And if she was to replace everything, it would have to be neat. With a surge of guilt which did not hold her back, she picked up the envelope and took out the magazines.

Startled by the front covers, shocked by the content of the magazine: ***Big Tits That Want it Hard.*** Almost afraid to look but overwhelmed with curiosity she flicked through the magazine. Topless, dyed blonde, big breasted women in all sorts of sexy positions. Some women were tied up and there was an unsavoury streak of S&M. She felt her own breasts, they were pert and soft. She thought he liked them. Was this his fantasy?

She threw the magazines on the floor. Did he think of this when they made love? She felt prudish and insecure. She had tried so hard to be perfect, to satisfy his every need but in his mind were these sluttish, topless women. Were these the women he craved, wasn't she enough for him? She worked so hard to look good. Was this really what turned him on? She felt her sexual confidence diminish into a small pile of broken rubble.

Standing up from the bed, she shut her eyes and tried to contain her sadness. She had a strong impulse to vomit then to run out of the apartment and never to return. She felt ashamed of her naïveté – she liked to consider herself a vixen but this was just too much. Max, she thought. Do I know you? He'd never displayed any hint of interest in this sort of thing. He had never complained before. Or maybe she hadn't noticed. She checked the dates of the magazines; the latest was eighteen months ago but why hadn't she seen them before? Boyish fantasies she thought. This wasn't Max. A friend probably bought them for a joke. But if this wasn't Max – why would they be in his drawer? It's just a joke – a friend put them there to shock her. Not her Max. It was probably his friend Andre. Andre from the agency. She never liked him. He looked at her in a way she found distasteful. Just because he didn't have Celeste, didn't mean she would make up for that. Ever. Did Max talk about her?

She looked around the apartment, contemplated her potential life with him. The security he offered to her as a wife and father to their children. He loved her. She loved him. They were ideal. Of course they were. Silly to argue over a stupid magazine with silly women. She was much more beautiful than them. With renewed understanding and tolerance, she looked at the magazines again. More closely this time and without prejudice or indignation. She was the sex kitten and so much better looking than these fat and ugly women.

However she was still disappointed with Max but more disappointed with Andre who was still the villain; she replaced the magazines back in the drawer. She would never go to that drawer again, in fact any private areas in Max's apartment. It was his space not hers. She was there by default not by invitation. She had no right to look and certainly no right to confront over something she had not been requested to see. This was Max's room and nothing in it was her business. Perhaps the maid found them at the back of a cupboard and discreetly put away. Yes, it was the maid. Or Andre. The magazines were there by accident.

She emptied the shopping, neatly put the food in the fridge and cupboards and started to scrub and sanitize the immaculate and pristine apartment. Ironic as she never cleaned at home and always had domestic help. As she began to tire from her exertions, she picked up the photograph of Max's grandfather Edward, in Germany. Max and his grandfather looked similar, a strong family resemblance. Same blond hair, tall stature, light-blue eyes and largish nose. Both had the same definitive jaw and wide shoulders which afforded great head and shoulder photographs.

Grandfather and grandson, she hated clichés but trees and apples came to mind. Max was a descendant from such a wonderful family and he was lovely too. The old man looked so kind and gentle. Like Max… the man she wanted to marry and with whom she wanted to have children. Edward was getting old and they had never met. How could she not meet him before he died? Everything and everybody special to Max was important to her too. It was part of his heritage, his history and the lineage which would be nurtured from her womb and which would be continued through their children.

She had never really considered herself as maternal before or perhaps the instincts had been suppressed. For her sex was about fun and pleasure but as she considered the future, she saw the wider possibilities and realities. It felt good, something inside suddenly felt mature as if deep within, an instinct was blossoming into a beautiful

flower. Life within her, the thought of making life through love…
with Max. She could not wait to meet his grandfather during their
forthcoming trip to Prague. Proudly she replaced the photograph on
the shelf. Not looking, she misjudged it and the photograph dropped
on the floor. The back of the frame opened and the photograph fell
out. It was no longer perfect but it didn't matter.

      After she had finished the cleaning, she took a hot shower to
wash off her exertions. She wiped herself, dried her hair and then
crept into his bed, curled up on the left-hand side. Shuffling between
the crisp sheets, she felt relaxed from the scent; closed her eyes and
imagined Max beside her. His hands on her shoulders then down her
back, between her thighs and caressing her intimately. She imagined
the warmth of his body beside her, strong arms which made her feel
secure, content and safe. Enjoying the moment, peace and quiet in a
comfortable large bed, she closed her eyes and allowed herself to
drift into a light but refreshing sleep. So Max liked a certain fantasy,
perhaps she might indulge him. That would surprise him and rather
like Scheherazade, you're more likely to keep a man interested if
you keep him on a cliff-hanger of possibilities and endings. And
although her life did not depend upon surviving the next day but
perhaps her relationship did…

      Max sat on the bed and watched Portia sleep. She looked so
peaceful and child-like in her slumber. She sensed his presence and
woke up with a start. "Max – how long have you been here?"

      "Not long, just watching you." He bent over and kissed her
gently on the lips. She looked so comfortable in his bed. At first he

was annoyed to find her sleeping there but the softness of her perfume, her pretty clothes on his chair, it was a welcome sight and he felt moderately aroused. He contemplated *taking her* as she slept. Gently so as not to awaken her. But if she did awake it might have been difficult to explain.

He stroked her soft face and she smiled back, tired eyes with a hint of passion in their gaze. "I've missed you" she murmured with a slight pout.

"You look beautiful. So vulnerable. I was going to make love to you as you slept. But then I wouldn't have seen your sexy eyes."

She smiled, "But that wouldn't be much fun for me" she teased as she raised a seductive eyebrow.

"Yes but I'd have enjoyed it. Screwing a dead woman."

She was puzzled by his response. Surely her pleasure was part of his? "A dead woman. Is that your fantasy?" She asked unable to contain her shock. She didn't want to tell him she felt physically repulsed.

"I have a lot of fantasies, some really naughty ones but they're not for the woman I love... But if you're interested in pretending, it would have given an interesting slant to our sex life." He bent over and kissed her but she didn't respond. She was open-minded to games, dressing up, pretending to be a nurse and things like that but a dead woman? She thought of the magazines.

His hand went to her neck then her breast. Pulling down the sheet, he looked at her breasts, bent over and kissed them. Gently biting on her nipple she tried to resist him but felt herself

57

involuntarily responding. She moaned with slight pleasure and simultaneous annoyance and pain. It was difficult to be angry with him. His other hand was gently caressing the curve of her slight physique, hesitant at her stomach as if teasing her with the potential of pleasure or pain if her desires were not fulfilled. She was clearly relaxed and her initial resistance was beginning to falter. She was responsive to his touch and aching for just that little bit more… He easily aroused her, she loved him. It wasn't hard to respond to his touch and he knew exactly what to do. He was just playing she told herself. Pretending. Teasing. Just trying to gauge a response from her but rising passions overwhelmed her initial reticence.

"So do you like finding me in your bed?" she whispered as lovers do, when intimate.

For fuck's sake, he thought. He wished she hadn't spoken. Lost in his thoughts her words had disturbed him; would have been great if she could have stayed quiet, taken the hint and just lay still, motionless.

"Yes, yes of course" he muttered back. He stood by the bed and moved his hand back to her breast and with the other hand, undid his trousers, dropped them, then lowered his pants and climbed into bed beside her. She was beginning to moan, her head tilted back with sensual pleasure. His left hand held both hands above her head, the right hand moved between her thighs. Involuntarily she parted her legs, exposed herself to him. Positioning his legs between hers, he felt inside her, massaged her inner folds, then finding her intricate and most delicate area, manipulated it with

58

his forefinger until she was writhing in pleasure… gasping… moaning and trying to push herself towards his body in her eager response to his deft technique.

Then slumped back, her brow sweaty, her voice throaty as she tossed her head from side to side. Beautiful eyes closed, body responding to his touch. He was aroused too but didn't want her to touch him. Holding her down, in one lunge he was inside her – she was wet, moist and as excited as a professional. He thought about the women in Prague and for a moment, pretended he was with one of them. He lunged deeper inside her concentrating on his own pleasure and the fantasy of a climax with an unknown stranger. One who responded because she was paid, not because she loved him. Who moaned because he controlled her emotions with cash. For the next five minutes he was in absolute control as he aggressively thrust himself inside her… pushing hard and manfully. He manipulated her mind, her body and her responses.

Moving slowly at first, he waited until he could feel her nails scratching his back. He moved quicker as she pulled at him; her moans were timed to his thrusts. So deep into her wet, intimate parts that controlled both their passions. She called out his name – told him she loved him. He ignored her as he focussed on fantasy. Her speaking killed the moment. At the point of orgasm he held on until it was impossible then exploded a steady stream of semen; ejaculating into her body, releasing himself of all tensions, worries and frustrations. It was intense, satisfying and he felt purged and great. Then he lay on his back, savoured the silence and physical respite from his sexual exertions.

Back to reality. Shit – he forgot to check if she had taken her contraceptive pill. Surely she had. But then he felt sick, she did keep bringing up marriage. But then he hated condoms so whether she did or didn't was her problem, not his.

Portia became twitchy, waiting for the obligatory post-sexual conversation. She turned over in the bed, stroked his arm but he didn't respond. "Do you love me?" she asked.

"Of course. Yes of course." He was angry she had broken the silence. She always disturbed his rest. Normally he would put his arm around her which avoided the need for inane chat. But this time he had forgotten as he was busy focusing on his own contentment rather than her emotional needs. Mental note: always embrace Portia after sex or tell her you love her. It seemed cold and heartless but he wasn't in the mood to talk, certainly not an in-depth conversation about their love and affection. Men just don't think like that. They don't need confirmation. He had just fucked her, why analyze? It seemed so fruitless and was such a waste of time and energy. Of course he loved her, he had said so…At some point.

Portia got out of bed, went into the bathroom and showered. Max closed his eyes and relaxed. At last some peace and quiet. He pretended he was back in Prague and the prostitute had left the bed to service another client. But she had been satisfied by him, he was the best lover she'd ever had. He fantasized her begging him to return the next day. He imagined arranging a meeting with her where he wouldn't need to pay for her services – simply because, he was the best. She wanted him for sex, not for love. Uninhibited and slave to her sexual passions and desires. He felt relieved, smiled, then spread out in the middle of the bed.

Portia returned to the bedroom, smelling like roses and her hair still damp from the shower. "I love you" she whispered.

"I love you too. And I'd also love a blow-job. So why don't you be a good little girl and suck my cock. I won't come in your mouth, just want to feel your tongue." He lay back on the bed and folded his arms behind his head. Smiling to himself as she lowered the sheet, she wiped him with a towel to clean him, then kissed the blondish hair on his chest and then moved her head downwards. He enjoyed the wet sanctuary of her mouth as her tongue licked him whilst she cupped and gently massaged his testicles.

Portia was rather disappointed with his tone but naturally, she dutifully obliged. She knew what he liked, when to suckle him with her mouth, tongue and when to swallow when or if he came.

Portia checked her diary, her period was two weeks late. Could it be possible despite her taking the pill? She went to a pharmacy before breakfast, picked up a pregnancy kit and tested herself. As she waited for the result she contemplated motherhood and what if? She felt secretly delighted that potentially, she might be pregnant.

She thought of her friend Celeste. Despite their emails and protestations to meet it hadn't happened. Now she was married to Jean-Pierre and had a baby. Celeste and Jean-Pierre Hughes. Portia felt very guilty, her dearest friend was now a mother. Had she been errant as a friend? It would be lovely to see her and also the little boy, Francois. She regretted that she hadn't gone to the wedding but Max had not been invited and it was difficult. So she had sent a poor excuse and a generous present. Everybody was happy. Well not everybody.

Despite feeling so happy about her relationship with Max, he hadn't proposed marriage and in her heart, she yearned for a child too. Tears welled up, she bit her lower lip to try and control her feelings. She ached for a child, so desperately wanted Max to commit and settle. Despite her privileged background compared to Celeste's working class parentage, ironically it was Celeste who had everything now. Celeste who had a devoted husband and family… Although she wasn't rich, she was happy…

Nervously she checked the result. Would Max want to marry her if she was pregnant? Would she have to have an abortion? Could she cope as a single mother? What did SHE want? She wanted a baby…

The result was negative. Portia pulled down the toilet seat, sat on it and cried bitterly. She felt so empty inside; barren and unfulfilled. These new emotions frightened her, she couldn't control or manipulate them. To develop her femininity was to embrace the fear of failure or being rejected. Could she bear that? Instead of a flat no, she briefly pondered the possibilities. Love without life? Or life without love? Not just from a man or men but from an infant nurtured from within. She touched her stomach, it felt flat and empty. She imagined it protruding with life. She cried for her loss even though she hadn't lost anything except a hope and possibility.

She tried to imagine a life as a wife and mother, having children, especially a little girl. A child to dress up, play with, take shopping, adore and spoil, like she had been. A little friend to take to afternoon tea, spend time with... she thought of her childhood, of Celeste and the fun they had as children. How they played, told each other their secrets and ultimately, grow-up together. She wanted a child to have the childhood she had enjoyed, surrounded by good friends, a lovely home, presents, girlish things... She had resented her parents because they weren't her birth parents but now, she realised that what they had offered her, was exactly what she would want her own children to enjoy too.

But she wasn't pregnant. This was still a fantasy and she was getting older. Was the proverbial biological clock ticking? She wanted to be a mother and she wanted Celeste back in her life. Had she really been so selfish that she had lost what was important before she had realized the worth? She thought of her mother Simone, and how she had ached for a child. That after her confirmation it would be impossible for her to conceive, she adopted a vulnerable and abandoned baby. For the first time ever, she understood that maternal ache that consumes and overwhelms with its desire – its insatiable need that trumps all other emotions. It becomes part of you, your whole body devoured by it. That everything seems to scream baby, child. You cry to hold a child, to feel the warmth of its little body against yours. That your heart is open and wounded, you're bleeding with internal pain because you're empty... Could she love a child that wasn't hers? Yes she could. Her eyes filled with tears, it felt as if it was the first time ever, she understood, craved or needed real and true love.

Chapter 4

"Hello Max. I haven't heard from you. Are you well?"

"Morning grossvater. Sorry, I was asleep..."

"Asleep, it's 8.30 a.m. You should be up and enjoying the day." His tone was stern and non-negotiable. For a man in his late eighties, he was always up at 5 a.m. and ready to start the day.

"Look. Can I call you back?" Max asked. He wasn't in the mood to defend his morning in bed with Portia.

"Do you have a woman with you?" His grandfather asked teasingly. "Perhaps. Perhaps somebody special." Max hated discussing his personal life with his grandfather. It just didn't feel right and despite his grandfather's insistence that he had led a *vibrant* life, Max just couldn't imagine it. His grandfather certainly appeared to be astute but Max look for signs of mental deterioration. His body was riddled with arthritis and his hands shook from Parkinson's disease. It was sad that his mental agility facilitated an absolute awareness of his physical fragility; his body was slowly collapsing as his mind gauged each degenerative step.

He heard his grandfather breathe deeply as if in thought. "Don't forget what I told you. Some women you marry. Some are for fun. They're not the same. Trust me Max, an old man's words of wisdom. There are two types of women and you don't waste your time with women who are worthless."

"Passé grossvater. Please, times have changed." He loved his grandfather but would not trust him with details of his love and sex-life. Albeit he couldn't help but be influenced by his grandfather's wisdom. He would just never admit to it.

Portia was as perfect as any woman could be. As long as she understood when to be serious and when to play, everything he wanted could be comfortably wrapped up with her as his no. 1 despite an unknown number of others. Why tell her? She would only get upset. The ideal of one man with one woman – equal respect and status – was what most men and women wanted from long-term relationships. Open relationships had to be agreed by both parties and not be just one-way. Portia would never have agreed. The difference now was Max played the game and was discreet with his adventures.

"Listen Max" his grandfather said sternly. "And the words of an older man who's been around a lot longer than you. Some women are for fun. Some are the types you marry. Your grandmother was a very special woman. A wonderful wife, mother and grandmother. Faithful, loyal and honest. Trusting. I still miss her daily. I feel she is still with me. Always with me. She had true virtues and values. You need a woman like this. Other women are for other things that men need."

"You make grandma sound more like a pet…"

"Show your grossmutter some respect."

"Are you?"

"Yes. She knew. We never discussed it. My relationship with you is different – you're my grandson and a man. I loved your grandmother, but you know…"

"No - I don't want to know."

"As you want Max. Call me when you have time. I would like to talk to you about some things."

"I'll call you over the weekend. We'll be seeing you soon. You remember we're going to Prague for a few days but thought it would be good to see you in Munich then to catch the train. My girlfriend Portia is insisting. Would be good for you to meet her."

"You love her?"

"In a manner of speaking. I suppose I do."

"That's good. But don't let her manipulate you. I sense she wants to meet us. I don't feel this meeting has been organised by you. Despite you being my grandson. Perhaps she is getting bored of you and wants an older man?"

"No. Portia would give you a heart attack. Trust me" Max teased but he resented his grandfather making a sexual comment about her. He knew his grandfather would comment on her beauty.

"Prague" his grandfather repeated with interest. "Beautiful city, I remember it well. Did you find that little hotel in Na Porici

66

that I mentioned. Very elegant. I spent some time there, many years ago when I was a very young man. A youth" then his voice trailed off and there was silence.

"Yes, Portia found the hotel you mentioned. It was just right. She prefers small and boutique rather than 5* hotel chains where all rooms are the same. Hotel Art Deco, we'll be staying there. Thank you for recommending it."

"You didn't need to stay there, I was just saying, I remember it. Didn't know it was still there."

"Yes, looks very nice and not too far from the Square either. A good location."

"Good and I look forward to seeing you."

Max smiled: "Of course." He loved his grandfather as a mentor; he saw more of him than his own father. He had grown up under his influence and direction and Max respected and admired him, wanted to be like him. His grandfather was a wonderful and fair man. Somebody who was decent, caring and devoted to his family despite his outside interests.

Munich

As they arrived into Munich, Portia was fascinated by the airport building. Feeling more like a giant glass house than an airport, it was pristine to the point of feeling sterile. Max was more concerned about getting a taxi to their hotel then to take in the view.

Luckily there was a short queue for taxis. "Hotel Vier Jahreszeiten"

"Would he know the address?" Portia asked. Both the taxi driver and Max laughed. "You never told me what hotel; you said it would be a surprise. I don't know."

"Absolutely he would" Max replied. But rather than patronize her any further, he added: "Maximilianstrasse 17." The taxi driver nodded politely but smiled in the driver's mirror to Max.

"Knowing you Max, it's beautiful."

"Yes and I know you'll be comfortable." He gave her that wry smile which meant he knew something she didn't. Munich had never really appealed to Portia before but she did like Budapest and certainly Vienna, so perhaps Munich would add a certain charm and aspect to her worldliness. She was open to the possibilities plus she had heard the shopping was outstanding! Every good shopping area was Portia territory. The short holiday was beginning to feel rather good.

"We'll relax first from the journey and then enjoy a sumptuous dinner at the Restaurant VUE Maximilian… then perhaps an early night? Tomorrow we'll see my grandfather for lunch."

"I look forward to meeting him. You talk more about him than any other member of your family. Would I be wrong in assuming that by meeting your grandfather, it somehow means you take me seriously too? Looking for his approval?"

Max smiled. "You know I'm very fond of you but let's not rush things."

She hid her disappointment well. "We don't need to rush. And anyway, somebody else might whisk me off my feet and you'd have lost your chance."

He grabbed her around the waist and pulled her close to him: "You'll never find a lover better than me, so would always come crawling back."

"Crawling. I don't think so."

"I do." Gently he touched her knee then started to move his hand up her skirt. "I know your little secrets. Know what you like. So why would you leave?"

"Stop it" and she playfully slapped his hand. The taxi driver was watching them in the driver mirror and was amused by the spectacle. He had seen it all as a taxi driver; even people having sex in the back of his cab.

Portia flushed. Max smiled at the taxi driver who pretended not to have noticed.

Arriving to the hotel, Portia was incredibly impressed with Maximilianstrasse. Omega, Louis Vuitton, Versace: Maximilianstrasse certainly had potential for being a favourite city. Modern, clean, fresh cream and grey coloured buildings on a neat and uniform road. Wide like Champs Elysees but more modern. Everything about the long street was efficient and rather like the airport.

The hotel was magnificent and a wonderful example of a 5 star hotel at its best. The lobby had a marble floor, oak panelled walls and a happy, smiling, front of house team who made every guest feel like a valued family member. Paradise she thought and smiled to herself. Munich had certainly been elevated into her top tier of favourite cities. "I like it" Portia said to Max.

"I knew you would! That's why we're here."

However before Portia was to be let loose on the shopping, Max's intention was to loosen her clothes. Her attire before his wallet, he believed in upfront payments…

Portia and Max were looking at the lunchtime menus, when an elderly, frail looking gentleman approached their table. He balanced himself carefully on his walking stick. He was thin but his clothes fitted him well. He was stylish and looked elegant. Just as he approached Max, a shaft of light shone through the restaurant's large windows. He squinted and his lips tightened. "I think too bright for me" then he smiled at Portia.

"Grossvater" Max exclaimed then embraced his grandfather. They smiled tenderly at each other; the grandfather was clearly very fond of his grandson. He looked at Portia, smiled then nodded to Max.

"Your girlfriend is very beautiful. If I were ten years younger…"

"You mean fifty years younger" Max interrupted.

"Ah, give an old man a little grace. You could have at least agreed at twenty years! Plus the older men get, the younger we like our women. Let's compromise on thirty – how can I possibly compete with my grandson" and both men laughed.

"Portia, meet my grandfather, my grossvater, Edward Schultzmann." She stood up and extended her hand.

"Please my dear" and he kissed both her cheeks. "Such youth and beauty." His English was perfect but punctuated with a hint of a German accent.

Max helped his grandfather into the chair and then gently pushed it towards the table. Edward shuffled in the seat then settled as he felt comfortable. "It is wonderful to see you both here in Munich. Portia, do you like this wonderful city?"

"Yes. Well I like the shops. But don't you miss England?"

"Yes, of course. But my business interests brought me back to Germany, plus I grew up here. I still maintain a residence in Marble Arch but my visits to London are dwindling. Otherwise we would have met in London."

"Perhaps when you're next back?" she asked then looked at Max. She wondered why he had never told her about his home in London before.

"So let's drink a toast" and the old man gestured to the sommelier to bring over the wine menu. Without looking he selected a bottle of Moet & Chandon. Max was like his grandfather, the lively host who liked to order champagne.

"Are you happy with champagne?" Edward asked Portia.

"Yes. Yes please Mr. Schultzmann."

"Edward," he interrupted. "Please call me Edward."

He stared at her. At first it felt like an old man being kind but then something made her feel uncomfortable. From the corner of her eye, she could see him staring at her. His eyes were light blue, a bit like Max's, except his looked like sharks' eyes. Predatory. Piercing. As if they saw more than what they were looking at. She moved her head to face him and smiled. He nodded but kept his thoughts secret.

"So where in London are you from?" he asked her.

"Hampstead" she replied. "Well my parents live there, I am looking to buy my own place, perhaps near St. Johns Wood. So I could be near Max. That's assuming I'm never invited to stay with him" she teased.

For a moment, the grandfather imaged her on a table with her legs open. He wondered if Max took her roughly and whether she liked it. He looked at Portia as he fantasized about her. She sensed he was looking at her with sexual thoughts, so she turned around and smiled at Max for support.

Portia felt uncomfortable and poured a glass of water. "Edward, some water?" she offered.

"Please" he replied. Then made a point of touching her hand when he passed her the glass.

Max noticed and was not impressed. His grandfather had never behaved like this before. What had come over him he wondered? He was always a gentleman but there was a hesitancy that was slightly alarming. His last girlfriend was Dutch, Eva and Edward didn't give her a second look despite being more beautiful than Portia.

Max carefully read the menu. As it was in German, Portia wasn't sure what to order and didn't want to look parochial by asking for a translation. Max sensed her discomfort.

"Portia. Would you like chateaubriand with béarnaise sauce?"

"And perhaps a glass of Australian Cabernet Sauvignon to complement?" Edward intervened and recommended. "Some wine might help you to relax. You look tense my dear."

"I'm fine Edward" she replied. "It's been a long journey."

"Yes" he said quietly. "A long way from home."

Max laughed. "Travel is getting easier grossvater."

The atmosphere was not comfortable despite the pleasantries. Portia was keen to finish the meal as soon as possible. Despite Max's enthusiasm about his grandfather, there was something decidedly strange about his behaviour.

The wine was served and Max afforded Edward the privilege to examine the label, check the cork and then taste. Edward nodded, the wine was in perfect condition. A waiter then served the aperitif: A small bowl of tomato soup and pork crackling. "Bon Appetit" Max declared and they started to eat.

The chateaubriand was sumptuously presented. Max and Edward waited for Portia to start eating; she cut off a small piece and tasted; succulent and tender, the béarnaise sauce took the beef to another level of excellence. Edward cut off a larger piece and put it in his mouth. She was startled by his handling of the knife. The meat was tender and didn't merit too much cutting; however he cut too hard. He had come across as stylish and elegant, yet his handling of his food was in some ways, quite base. She looked over at Max, he wasn't watching his grandfather. He was enjoying the food and had just emptied a large glass of wine.

"Perfect choice grossvater," he said. "Really a good merlot." He drank some more.

The food was delicious and their individual appraisals of the meal dominated the lunch-time conversation. There were no more uncomfortable silences; the conversation was light and friendly. They talked about Munich, the imminent trip to Prague, life in general and Portia's plan for a concentrated shopping trip to the best shops in Munich. Edward was amused by her casual manner, her carefree approach to life. He wished he was so much younger; she like the others, would not have had a chance to refuse him.

Sitting back and enjoying a post-lunch coffee, Edward begun to look uncomfortable in his seat.

"I think we've been here too long grossvater" Max said. "Would you like us to walk you back to your apartment?"

"Yes – that would be good. Thank you. I'm an old man," he nodded to Portia. "And I'm not as healthy and fit as I used to be." She smiled politely but couldn't help wondering if perhaps, there was a nuance in his comment as if implying past grandeur and a catalogue of success.

Edward lived in a serviced apartment, five minutes from the hotel. They walked slowly to his residence and waited patiently as his shaky hands struggled to put the key in the lock. He was muttering something in German. Then the key turned and they entered into the hallway. Comfortable and elegant, minimalist in its décor, classical furniture and a few ornaments and books. As Portia walked around the room, she looked at the photographs. Pictures of Edward and his wife Anna. In one picture, Anna was dressed up and clearly going somewhere special. As she picked it up and looked closely, she noticed Anna was wearing a beautiful brooch: A jewelled panther. It was approximately the same size and workmanship as her snake. Diamond eyes and something in the curves which gave it a feeling of movement. She held the photograph close to her face and examined it carefully.

She didn't hear Edward appear behind her. "Lehr " he told her. "Pretty isn't it. I can see you examining it."

"Yes. Very unusual. Can I see it?" She asked him.

He grimaced. "It was stolen."

"Oh! I'm sorry. Your wife must have been upset."

"Yes she was. But I was lucky and through my work, was able to procure other things for her."

"Procure?"

"Yes. Procure. But these are demons from the past. I liked this photograph because Anna looks very beautiful. It was after this party, that I asked her to marry me. The brooch was a gift of love. If she took the brooch, she agreed to give me her heart in return." Portia wondered if she should ask him about her brooch. Her instinct told her to keep quiet, despite a strong temptation.

"That's a beautiful story. It's a shame you don't have it."

"As I said, it was stolen. Do you know Ulrich Lehr? His work?" he asked.

"Not really. On my first date with Max, we went to an exhibition in London? You have obviously influenced his interest in jewellery."

"I personally introduced him to Oscar Heyman as a company of course. The man himself died in 1970." Edward nodded with pride. "Yes, beautiful work. It is nice for a grandfather to share his interests with his grandson. It's a special relationship, a grandfather and grandson. Better than a son – somehow more powerful. Your grandson goes into the future in a way that we old people cannot share. Our blood and on our behalf into the future. Very special."

Our blood echoed through her mind. How he touched the raw nerve that haunted her. And whose blood was she? She paused and was immediately sad and pensive.

"I had this brooch in my pocket and Anna found it. So we made a pact, if she really wanted it, I had to have something in return. Which tells you that you must always check clothes before going to the laundry or throwing away? You may find something precious. Or you may 'procure' something precious. Anna was also worried it was destined for another woman. By offering it to her, reassured her that she was my true love."

"Perhaps I should check Max's pockets. So I can 'procure' something."

"I don't think you could procure my dear. I'm sure you would earn it." He looked at her suggestively. He was making a point. "Tell me Portia, are you interested in fashion, history and style?" He asked changing the subject. "Looking at you, I would assume you are. Mrs. Simpson was very stylish and interested in beautiful 1930s jewellery. Do you know much about her?" He held her gaze longer than would be considered customary.

"Yes of course. Part of my history studies. And her husband the king, another Edward. He abdicated – they said because of his love for her. But perhaps there was a sinister political allegiance too?"

"Perhaps. Who knows? And after all these years, does it matter?"

Portia wondered if Edward had a mistress. Whether the brooch had been for her but Anna had accidentally found it. As for Mrs. Simpson's sense of style; Portia really wasn't interested.

"Where did you get it from? Who was the original owner?"

"Who and when?" he repeated, then hesitated as he contemplated his answer. "A kind man gave it to me. But as I have just said, this is history."

Then he took the photograph and put it in a drawer and not back on the mantelpiece. "Perhaps we shouldn't discuss this anymore" and Portia nodded.

"You must be tired. Max and I should go now, let you rest. It's been such a lovely lunch and I feel honoured to have met you. Max talks about you often, now I can visualize the face and the person, behind the legend." She remained polite but was keen to leave.

Edward composed himself, took her hand and kissed it. "You are very kind. And Max is very lucky to have such a beautiful young woman to adorn his arm. I am honoured to have met you."

She didn't like Edward . She had a sick feeling in her stomach being near him. When he touched her, cold shivers went up and down her spine. His hands were perfect, his nails were manicured but there was something not right. They were too perfect, not like a man's hands, they looked crooked and he had big knuckles. They made him look like a cripple.

Max embraced his grandfather; Portia kissed him on both cheeks.

"Isn't he great despite being a bit strange but he's getting old." Max said when they were leaving the building.

"He's a kind and wonderful man. Thank you for introducing me to him."

"You know he really liked you. I've never seen him so taken with a woman before, especially my girlfriends." Max paused for thought. "He was certainly very comfortable with you, relaxed. I can see he liked you. Liked talking with you."

"That's good," she replied but didn't feel the same. She was trying to appease Max in order to appeal to his gentler side.

"I was looking at a photograph and noticed a brooch shaped like a panther. Apparently it was special. Do you know much about it?"

"I didn't know there was a panther brooch. I don't think I've ever seen it. You see, already he trusts you with things that he hasn't told me."

"No. It doesn't matter. Just that I had the feeling it had particular sentimental value. Your grandmother was wearing it in a photograph."

"Ah, the photograph on the table. I had never noticed the brooch."

"I don't know why but he put it in a drawer and away from view. "I was surprised that if he liked the photograph as much as he said, why put it away?"

"I really don't know," Max replied beginning to feel bored of Portia's analysis.

"Prague tomorrow Portia. We need an early night. Plus you look gorgeous in that dress and I'd rather like us to have a night of uninhibited sex. What do you think? I've had a stressful week and I'd like YOU to sort that out. Sex in Munich followed by sex in Prague. Plus of course, we need to fit in a little bit of time for some shopping to keep you happy. Well happy outside of the pleasure I give you."

Back at the hotel, they undressed and showered together.

"The bedroom is beautiful Max. I'd like us to make love in it. Really become intimate in this trip, get to know each other better. Thank you again, for introducing me to your grandfather. It means a lot to me."

"I needed to see him. You don't need to keep thanking me. Anyway, let's have some fun later. We're relaxed, away from the stresses of work, I could really do with a long, hard session. Are you in the mood?"

If she had been in the mood – she wasn't anymore but she indulged him. She was good at faking it and he was too involved with his own pleasure to notice her own, unsatisfied desires.

The following day and as planned, they took the train from Munich to Prague. It was a six hour train ride and the views were very pretty. Max looked relaxed and content. The trip had lost its romance. There were times when the relationship just felt cheap. She felt as if she was just there for 'the ride'. A bedroom companion that was tolerated during the daytime. Why did he feel the need to be so mean? Why didn't he just show some tenderness rather than making her feel base and crude? Whenever she felt they were getting close he held back and was nasty. Why did he so regularly disappoint?

The hotel taxi collected them from Prague train station. The chauffeur held up a board with their names written clearly in big, black letters:

MR. AND MRS. MAX SCHULTZMANN
HOTEL ART DECO, PRAHA

The board looked so formal as if Prague welcomed their arrival. Especially the names, Mr. and Mrs. Max Schultzmann . It looked perfect as if they were two halves of the same surname. Perhaps things would be better in Prague. Perhaps Max had organised the names to surprise her… "I'll be dealing with the manager when we get there. I never said we were Mr. and Mrs."

"But it does look rather good Max. Don't you think?"

"Not to me."

She punched him playfully but his words shattered her illusion of them being a couple.

Portia and Max walked in silence towards the limousine. The chauffeur took their cases and put them into the boot of the car. They climbed into the back and Portia cuddled up to Max. He seemed uncomfortable and shuffled. She retreated to her half of the back seat. She was so desperate for reassurance of their relationship. Max just didn't see the signs.

"Oh Max, don't you feel remotely romantic?" She tried to look cute, opened her eyes widely and stroked his arm.

"Come on Portia. It's been a long morning, getting up early and a long train journey, I said we should have flown. I'm just a bit tired. You know I get grumpy when I'm tired. Do you mind if I just shut my eyes 'til we get to the hotel."

"Yes, but you could make an effort" she retorted. Crossing her arms and looking sadly out of the window, she didn't want him to see the tears in her eyes.

He shut his eyes and lent against the window. She looked at the views outside of the car window. Staring into space, she was oblivious of the houses, the cars, that first image of Prague as they

81

drove into the city. Her eyes were open but she didn't see anything. Just felt the pain inside at his rejection of her touch.

The driver called the hotel just before they arrived. The doorman and receptionist waited at the entrance and warmly welcomed them into the hotel. The lobby had a brown, stone coloured tiled floor, a large Art Deco Tiffany light fitting and bronze ornaments. A large painting of a woman in a red flowing dress was hung behind the concierge's desk. As they walked down the few steps into the reception, Max nearly tripped as he was still tired from his rest and hadn't completely woken up.

The hotel was beautiful, yet Portia sensed something quite sinister; coldness sent a shudder down the nape of her neck. She looked around the reception in case there was an open window, a draught, something that could justify that cold chill. All the windows were closed. In the far corner was a closed door. She wondered what was inside and walked over to it.

"Madame" the concierge called. "That's private – for staff only." She removed her hand from the handle and walked back towards the desk. The concierge was a middle-aged man with grey hair. He seemed to change from a position of professional friendliness to aggressive firmness within a nanosecond. Portia didn't enquire further. His tone made it clear that it was non-negotiable. Portia glanced over her shoulder at the door and looked back at the concierge.

They completed the registration forms, home details, passport numbers and the credit cards slips for a deposit. Keys in the form of plastic cards were passed to each of them in a neat little envelope with the hotel's address and phone number.

"Welcome to Hotel Art Deco and on behalf of the hotel's management, we hope you will enjoy your stay in Prague."

"Yes, I'm sure we will" Max said as he took both keys. "Beautiful hotel, when was it built? Early 1900s?"

"1897 and was very popular with the Prague literati. The hotel was totally refurbished in 2000 to its present state now and its original glory."

"And so, Mr. and Mrs. Schultzmann" then he looked down at their registration forms, "I apologise, Mr. Schultzmann and Miss D'Allegro I am pleased to inform you that we have given you our best suite." He waited for a response or some level of enthusiasm. There was silence. "Would you like a map of Prague?" He then picked up two maps and handed each of them a large foldable map. "Enjoy your stay....Next" the concierge called. And the French couple behind them in the queue started their formalities. The doorman took Max's and Portia's suitcases and gestured them to follow him.

The halls were quite narrow, dark and badly lit. The doorman, Max and Portia walked in silence towards the room. The doorman paused, checked the door number then opened the door, turned on the lights with the key and showed Portia and Max, the bathroom, bedroom, safe and view which overlooked the street.

The room was beautiful; a stone coloured marble bathroom with brass taps, a large king-sized bed dominated the baroque styled room. It was ornately furnished with green heavy, curtains and tasselled tie-backs. A round coffee table, obligatory television, coffee-making machine, concealed fridge and prints of the Vltava River and Charles Bridge.

"I don't think we'll be needing the television" Max stated.

"I thought you were tired" Portia replied.

"Oh I hope you're not going to be moody. We're here now, relax, I feel better."

Portia smiled but her enthusiasm for a romantic interlude upon their arrival had subsided. His rebuke of her touch in the car had upset her. Also, there was something sinister about the room. A dark foreboding, a tangible eerie sensation; chillness despite the room being heated and warm. Perhaps it was the lobby? She still felt quite alarmed and aware of her surroundings as if her protective instincts were at full alert. She felt the adrenalin, her heart beating just that bit faster. Aware of sounds, echoes, shadows. Her eyes wide and alert she felt her senses sharpen.

Trying to relax, she went into the bathroom, ran the hot water for a long bath and added some hotel bath and shower gel. It didn't have a scent, just the normal hotel accessories which fulfilled a basic need but didn't have the luxury of a named brand. She regretted not bringing her own. Some rose or jasmine would have calmed her mood.

Max relaxed in the bedroom, she heard him turn on the television, she heard cheers as he had obviously chosen a sports channel. She didn't bother to lock the door, the room already felt claustrophobic. The mirrors began to mist from the hot steam. She outlined a smiley face on the misted tiles. Despite her cynicism of the bath gel, they did produce an excessive amount of bubbles and the room felt calm. Removing her clothes, she gently climbed into the bath; the water was very hot and her white skin went a dark pink from the heat. Slowly she lowered into it and her body quickly adjusted to the temperature. Tying her hair into a ponytail, she used the hotel's shower cap to secure her hair and a small flannel, damp with cold water to place upon her forehead and across her eyes.

Portia tried to relax. The room was hot and misty. She heard the door open; a faint draught came in from the bedroom. "Max... I'm relaxing" she said without removing the flannel. Then she heard him laughing in the bedroom. She opened her eyes and looked at the door. It was shut. I must have dozed she thought then wiped her face with the flannel. It had lost its coldness from the hot room. Running it under the bath tap, she refreshed it and laid it again on her forehead as she sat back in the bath.

She thought of this trip and her relationship with Max. Would this mini-break symbolize anything she wondered? The warm water made her feel secure as if cozy within a mother's womb. Safe. Secure. Protected. She lifted up the flannel and looked over at the door, it was firmly shut. Then chillness again, seemed to float across her then towards the ceiling. Despite being alone, she didn't feel it. She lowered herself beneath the water, so her breasts wouldn't be exposed. Although tempted to close her eyes, she didn't and the bubbles made her eyes sting. The light was on so perhaps an extractor was working. She tried to reassure herself but was not convinced. She rubbed her body with the gel and started to wash herself. Singing gently she shattered the silence which seemed foreboding.

"How long are you going to be?" Max called. "I need to use the toilet."

"Not long, just a few more minutes. I want to shower off the bubbles."

"Need some help?" he teased. But she could tell by his tone, he didn't mean it. A few seconds later, he cheered when clearly another goal had been scored. He was engrossed in whatever match he was watching.

As she stood up to shower, naked and alone in the bathroom, she again felt that cold, chilling air. She looked around the room for the origins of the draught but couldn't see anything. The door was shut, there wasn't a window and any holes or gaps in the tiling.

"I'm going to the lobby Portia. I need to use the bathroom. Don't rush your bath."

She heard him leave, the door shut loudly behind him. She wanted to call out for him to wait but he had already gone. She was alone in the bathroom and room. Quickly she showered then covered herself with a large, white bath sheet and went into the bedroom. There was nobody else there but she didn't feel alone. Putting on the television, she selected a film from the movie channel. Filling the room with voices was preferable to the oppressive silence. She started to unpack her clothes and personal items but was not comfortable, so instead took out a night shirt, put it on then climbed into the bed. It was still light outside and eagerly, she waited for Max's return. She didn't like being in the room on her own. She pulled the duvet close to her face and peeked out from inside the large, king-sized bed.

She heard somebody outside of the door, a key put into the slot then Max appeared. Carrying an ice-bucket with a bottle of champagne. "Well my dear Portia. Let's start this weekend with a bang... In all senses." He opened the bottle then poured two full glasses of champagne. "To Prague and to us." He gulped down the entire contents of the glass then poured himself another. "And to us enjoying Prague and each other." He gulped that glass down too. Portia left her glass on the side and just watched him. She knew he drank with his artsy friends but not like this in front of her. Generally their drinking was more recreational. Clearly, he just wanted to get drunk.

"Please Max. Don't I intoxicate you enough?"

"Obviously not my dear." He touched her cheek, moved the duvet down and touched her shoulder. "You're still warm from the bath... Or should I say hot." He finished the third glass of champagne and poured himself another.

Portia watched him remove his clothes. He bent down and kissed her lips but not passionately. It was as if they were strangers. She tried to shake her head. With his left hand, he held her hands tight above her head. With his right, he held her face straight, clutching her jaw, pushing his fingers into her cheeks. Then he kissed her again. She tried to resist but her actions seemed to excite him more. He had held her down before but this felt different.

"Stop Max, this isn't nice."

"I think it is. We're just having a little fun here. Relax and enjoy yourself."

"You've had too much to drink."

He laughed: "Too much. Three glasses. I don't think so." Pushing her face deep into the pillow, he kissed her aggressively and bit her lip. She felt it bleed. With his right hand he moved it towards her right breast. He cupped it and then pinched her nipple so it hurt. She tried to call out but couldn't speak, his mouth clenched onto hers. She tried to struggle but in vain. He was stronger than her and she couldn't resist. Then he pulled the duvet down and pulled her nightshirt up, exposing her body.

"You ready for it?" he asked her. Or rather demanded. He looked eerily like his grandfather. She felt for a moment as if she was with Edward not with Max. That same expression. Those piercing blue eyes full of intent, staring at her but seeing through her as if she didn't exist.

"Stop Max…" he hit her across the face. Her face stung and reddened from the slap. "Please. Stop."

"Nope. Don't deny it, you do like it a bit rough don't you?"

"NO."

Putting his hand between her thighs, he parted her lips and roughly inserted some fingers inside of her. It hurt and she wanted to cry out. She tried to struggle. "Bit dry my dear. Isn't our little game enough to excite you?" He pushed harder and faster in an attempt to arouse her. She was clenched and frightened.

"NO. Max please…"

Then roughly he massaged her most sensitive areas, not sensually and gently but roughly so it hurt. "Come on, don't fight me here. You like my fingers up you, so I'm doing what you like. Want it a bit rougher?"

"Please Max NO." Releasing her hands, he quickly leapt on top of her then lunged inside. She was frozen in shock and fear. "Ah this is nice. This is nice. You're still a bit dry but just wet enough for me to get my cock up there."

"Please Max. Stop. NO."

He didn't listen as she tried to push him off. He grabbed both hands and clamped them at her sides. "Just relax. Enjoy yourself. Enjoy yourself. Stop being such a prude."

Portia tried to cut off, looked around the room, stared at the ceiling wishing the next five minutes to be over. Again that chill. That cold air which seemed to swamp. This time it didn't waft upwards but seemed to be around Max. His face contorted with pleasure, he didn't look like Max. He looked like a stranger.

"Yes," he shouted. "Come you fucking whore." He pushed deeper, his body weight thrown down harshly onto her gentle frame was painful. She felt herself bleeding from his exertions. She couldn't move, just lay there feeling like a victim of some vicious activity, a rape, an assault. "I'm coming" he shouted. "Oh yessss,

I'm coming," then he paused as he ejaculated then immediately withdrew. Dripping down his phallus and onto her thighs.

He rolled off and lay on his back. "That was fucking good." He was sweating and breathing deeply.

Portia's lip bled. Her breasts begun to bruise, her vagina and thighs sticky from sperm. Marks around her wrists where he had help her so tightly. Without speaking, she went back into the bathroom, showered and was too frightened to cry. Huddled in the bath, she stayed there until she heard him snoring in the bedroom.

They sat in silence at the breakfast table. Max ate his toast hungrily and slurped his coffee. She had never noticed him eat like this before. Like a hunter after a kill. His whole demeanour seemed to have changed. Sometimes he liked it a big rough but last night was in a league of its own. Yesterday's sexual escapade was of sorts, rape. Was it rape? It was – she had repeatedly said NO, so why was she sitting with him at breakfast, watching him tuck into his breakfast like a wolf.

Portia didn't touch the food or drink. She felt as if she sat opposite a stranger.

"What's wrong Portia?" he asked. "Your lip looks a bit sore" and he pointed to her lower lip. "Is it difficult to eat. Perhaps we'll go to the pharmacy and pick up a cream or something." Then he buttered another piece of toast and put a rasher of greasy bacon onto it. As he ate, his lips looked greasy.

He had no idea of her pain. The attack in the bedroom wasn't consensual. She hadn't agreed to that... a rough and aggressive foreplay, his penetration of her before she was ready. So many thoughts filled her mind. Disgust, concern, repulsion whilst Max continued to tuck into his breakfast.

"You're very quiet Portia. What's wrong?" he asked without interest.

"I'm not entirely sure we should discuss it in public Max."

"I don't understand" he stated as a matter of fact.

Portia wanted to cry. Did he really not know? Plus the incident in the bathroom with that cold draught. She had wanted to discuss it with him and although he would probably have just dismissed, that would have been enough reassurance. She was scared and needed some comfort.

The waiter brought over the coffee pot, looked into her cup and saw the coffee was still there. Cold. "Madame, some fresh coffee?" he asked politely. It was the only kind gesture she had received all morning.

"Yes please. A fresh cup" she responded. She didn't really want the coffee but she wanted the interaction. She wanted the waiter to pour her a coffee. "Thank you" she said politely and he smiled and nodded. Moving to the next table, she heard him offer another guest some fresh coffee. But for a few seconds, his invitation had put something human back into the morning.

She added the milk and a spoon of sugar. "Not too much sugar" Max whispered, his mouth still full of food. "You'll get fat." She added another spoonful, even though she normally only had one.

He looked displeased, she picked up the coffee and sipped at the hot beverage. It was too hot to drink and it burnt her sore lip. But it wasn't about the coffee. It was about defiance and an attempt at assertion when last night she had felt trapped.

Back in the bedroom, Portia sat in silence on the chair. She combed her hair as Max finished in the bathroom. When he came out, she eyed him angrily. "I didn't appreciate last night Max. I didn't like it at all."

"Oh don't be a prude," he teased. "I thought it was bloody fantastic. You were red hot and it was probably the best sex we've ever had. I liked what Prague did for you. Took away your inhibitions. Come on Portia. Don't be a spoil sport, it was just some fun. Well I enjoyed it. Probably enough for both of us. I think you've got a bit of a problem."

"If that's what you think – it was all in your mind. I kept saying NO."

"That was just part of the game – wasn't it?" He looked confused. "I thought you were enjoying it. The pretence at a struggle. I loved it. I loved you" he said unconvincingly. He felt guilty, something had come over him that he couldn't explain. Like a sinister incubus that possessed him and controlled his sexuality and physical demands. He knew it was a bit much but it felt so good at the time, he just couldn't help himself.

"Max, I wasn't playing. As for my pretence, you're stronger than me. You pinned me down. I didn't have a chance."

"Oh come on, it was just some fun." He walked over to her chair and stroked her face. Taking the brush, he brushed her hair and for a moment, seemed kind and loving. He took a lock of hair between his fingers and tenderly stroked it. She closed her eyes. This was her Max. Not the demon last night. "It was just some fun. We've been together a long time, it's good to spice up our sex life with something different. I wouldn't hurt you, I honestly thought you were enjoying it."

"Well perhaps next time, you might want to check with me first before you're so aggressive."

"Whoops" he laughed. "Got a bit carried away with the moment." Bending down he kissed her cheeks, then her nose, and then her mouth. She felt herself responding to his embrace, he sensitively caressed her breast. Feeling herself gasp in response, she was becoming sexually aroused.

Max carried her to the bed and made love to her; tenderly and passionately.

That afternoon was spent sightseeing Prague's historical and cultural sights. They walked to the Old Town Square and enjoyed a lunch at an open air café near the St. Mary of Tyn Church. The square was full of tourists, taking pictures, especially of the astronomical clock. The square was surrounded by buildings from all different eras. On the northeast side were from late 19th and early 20th century. A visual feast of different eras, designs and styles; neo classical, gothic, artistic and cultural. The city of Kafka; the capital of Bohemia. Prague astounded, excited and inspired.

Walking around the square, they found numerous shops selling Prague crystal. Portia noticed a very pretty red love heart on a red ribbon. Max bought it for her, together with matching earrings and bracelet. Although an economical alternative to her preferred jewellery, she felt these few pieces were a pretty souvenir from an exquisite city. She kept touching the glass, twisted the bracelet around her wrist. Looking at the wrist, the red marks were fading. The memory was fading.

Max had just had a lapse, a one-off episode that would never be repeated. It was probably the champagne, he had drunk too much. It had been an uncomfortable journey, he was probably dehydrated. The champagne had gone to his head. Made him behave differently. He didn't mean it, she thought. He loved her, he repeatedly told her so. She felt silly for bringing it up, making a business over it. It was just one episode and certainly not rape. She blushed at the thought. How could she ever think Max would rape her? They were in a loving, mature relationship. She was supposed to be open-minded. Max was right. She was being a prude. She remembered how she felt when she saw the magazines. She felt so confused. One minute a prude, the next game for anything. She wanted to be made love to but also wanted to be respected.

She linked her arm into his as they walked towards the river. "I'm sorry Max" she said. "I'm sorry I'm difficult sometimes." He smiled at her then looked out towards the Charles Bridge. "It's like the print in our bedroom."

"I didn't notice he replied. "I didn't see any pictures."

"Yes, on the wall next to the bed." He looked confused. "Sorry Portia, there aren't any prints in our room."

"There are" she laughed. "You just didn't notice because you were concerned with other things."

He looked angry and pulled away from her. "My perception is pretty sharp Portia. If there was a print, I'd have noticed it." He shook his head and thinned his lips.

"Oh perhaps you're right Max. Perhaps there isn't." But she knew there was but it wasn't worth another argument.

Portia and Max had spent most of the day doing the tourist trail around Prague. Museums, galleries, Prague Castle, Schwarzenberg Palace, fortunately both had brought comfortable shoes. Imperative in Prague where most of the roads are cobbled streets and certainly not geared to fashionable or uncomfortable footwear.

It had been a good day, the weather had been sunny and despite it being chilly, the sky was bright and the day felt crisp and interesting. Portia wanted a hot bath to wash off her exertions. Max lay on the bed as he waited for his turn in the bathroom. Portia was still smiling at the day. It had been such fun, they had drunk too much Pilsner, just sitting outside on the sidewalk watching people go by. Wondering about them, whether they were locals or tourists. One beer would become two, or sometimes three. Just sitting and resting their aching feet at a café for half an hour or even an hour. Going through the tour guide, trying to find their location, even when they had absolutely no idea where they were. It didn't matter. They didn't have an agenda or fixed itinerary. They didn't make any dinner reservations, didn't have any meetings; their time was their own and they just pottered around the city, trying to recognize strategic landmarks from the photographs in the book and taking it from there.

Max was relaxing from the stresses of the agency; he had let go of all that hyperactive pressure. He was more fun than she had remembered. Everything felt just wonderful. Would he propose she wondered? It seemed increasingly more likely. Plus she wanted him to.

They had drunk cold Pilsner beer, eaten goulash and bread dumplings. The food was stodgy and both Portia and Max felt a little unwell from the heavy food. They decided not to have dinner but to return to the hotel room and sleep off the carbs.

"If you need to use the bathroom, you better go now," she called. "Because I'm having a long, soak. I'll be a lobster from the hot water, then a prune from the cold. So if you need to go, now's your last chance for about half-an-hour." Portia began to run the water but Max didn't reply. She opened the door and saw him lying on the bed. Laid out on his back he was snoring with his mouth open. He was still wearing his shoes, arms spread out, he was clearly exhausted and also needed to sleep off the Pilsners!

Taking off her clothes and folding them up neatly next to the bathroom sink, she felt a draught again. She went back into the bedroom in case Max had gone out. He was still asleep on the bed. She tried to stop herself thinking about the night before. Remembered back to the better parts of the day, when they had both laughed and simply enjoyed being in each other's company. She tipped some bubble bath into hot water, made some circles with her hand and enjoyed the immediate response. The bath looked like a bubble-bath-bed; luxuriant, warm and very inviting. Gently she climbed in, the water was hot but very cozy. Laying in the bath, she covered her body with bubbles then closed her eyes.

Again she felt that cold wind. She opened her eyes and sensed another presence in the bathroom. "Max" she called. But there was no answer. "Max" she called out again. Again, no answer. As she laid in the bath, she didn't want to close her eyes again. Her senses were alert. Lying there, still, alone and naked, she felt very vulnerable and wanted to get out. But she was afraid to move, as if taking her attention away from an intense concentration of her surroundings would make her even more vulnerable.

She just stared at the walls, as if waiting for something to happen. She stared at the mirror, frightened to take her eyes away. Then she saw a shadow. She blinked in case her eyes were playing tricks. Perhaps she had stared for too long and her eyes were tired. Perhaps a bubble had fallen from her hair and blocked her vision. She wiped her head without taking her eyes off the mirror. Again, she saw a shadow. A dark outline, a shape. But she was alone in the bathroom. She wanted to call Max again but was afraid to move, speak or even breathe.

The shadow passed in front of the mirror then disappeared. A dark shadow reflected on the ceiling. She felt the cold wind go over her body. Her skin covered in goose-pimples; she was scared. The tap in the sink dripped some water; just a few drops but it was enough to make the sound eerily frightening. She knew there was a presence, she wasn't alone. Covering her body with the bubbles, she felt herself holding her breath.

Portia lay there for a few minutes; it felt like hours. Slowly she got out of the bath, covered her body with a towel and went into the bedroom. Max was awake, he stared at her; his expression unlike anything she had ever seen. It was Max – but it wasn't him. "Max?" she said quizzically. "What's wrong?"

He didn't answer but roughly took the towel off her body, threw her onto the bed and roughly forced her to have sex. Like the night before but this time it was worse. It was as if he was possessed by some sort of demonic entity. His body the shell for some evil spirit that controlled it. His eyes had a mad expression. He didn't speak as he handled her, it didn't feel normal; she felt like a vessel for his pleasure. He was a stranger in their bed. He didn't speak. Didn't say her name. Didn't kiss her.

Portia tried to fight him off but he was too strong. As she looked over his shoulder as he penetrated her from behind him, she saw a dark figure, a silhouette of a man in black. He didn't have a face, it was just a shape. A ghost.

She screamed out and tried to push Max off her. She was too weak. The shadow behind him didn't move. It just seemed to make the room darker as if it was suddenly nightfall. Her mouth was open but she couldn't utter a sound.

Then Max orgasmed and let out a loud, sigh of relief. The dark figure disappeared and Max rolled over onto his back. Breathing deeply, he wiped his phallus with the duvet cover. He was wet with sperm and blood where he had forced himself inside of her. She too felt blood slowly trickling down her thigh. Too scared to move she just lay on the bed, in shock and in fear. The dark figure had gone. The dark figure was satisfied with Max's performance.

She got off the bed and went back into the bathroom. She could hear Max's snoring, loud and satisfied. He was sprawled out on the bed as if it wasn't to be shared. His arms and legs open in the shape of a starfish. She went back into the bathroom and quickly showered off the residue from the despicable event. The figure had gone, she felt alone in the bathroom.

Then she went back into the bedroom, packed her things and without waking up Max, put the red Czech jewellery on the side cabinet, locked her case, took her passport, currency and documents from the safe. Then without looking back, she left the room, silently closing the door behind her. She went to reception, paid for the room, ordered a taxi and checked out of the hotel.

Chapter 5

Venice, Italy

From her Juliette balcony on the third floor of a grey, stone building on Salizzada Pio X, Celeste looked out onto the crowded street below. Vendors were selling their wares to an eager crowd of American tourists, she could hear them talking and bartering. People bartering for a Venetian mask, bric-a-brac, cheap Murano jewellery or a sailor styled sun hat with VENICE written in large letters across the brim. To her left, the majestic Rialto Bridge was instantly recognisable, white stoned and classically styled with uniform arches. Linking left to right of the Grand Canal, a Venetian, architectural icon.

"Come on Francois, let's go for a walk or perhaps you would like a little ride on the vaporetto?" But it was so hot and despite the cool breeze that the ride would have afforded, she decided to just stay local and perhaps to only venture out for an hour before returning for a light rest.

"There you go Francois, hold tight" and with one hand Celeste flicked open the pram and put her nine month old baby inside. She took out a largish sun hat from her bag to protect him from the bright sun, then tied her long, thick black hair into a tight bun. A few stray strands, hung either side of her face, framing her olive coloured skin. She didn't bother to check how she looked, it would do. She put on her sunglasses then noticed Mrs. Luigi from the flower shop walking past. "Buongiorno" she called as she lifted up her glasses so she could be recognized.

"Hello Celeste. Hello Francois" she replied. "What a beautiful boy – like his beautiful mother. And where is Francois going today?" He smiled, full of happiness and mischief. He liked Mrs. Luigi.

"Luig… Luig… play" he called.

"I think he wants to play" Celeste smiled. For a moment as his big eyes twinkled, she thought of the little boy at her school in Hampstead: Aldo. She wondered what he was doing and if he was happy.

"Yes, just for a little walk. Jean-Pierre will be home soon and I want to pick up some fruit. Plus Francois needs to get out of the apartment. He gets restless. You know babies."

"Yes. I love babies Celeste. Say 'hello' to Jean-Pierre for me. I'll tell Paolo that I saw you… that you all look, very, very well."

"Grazie Mrs. Luigi."

"Lovely boy. Such a lovely little boy. And today…. Bella giornata. Where are you going to get your things?"

"To the Rialto market."

"So enjoy this beautiful day. Ciao Celeste. Arriverderci Francois."

"Goodbye. Ciao." They embraced then went their separate ways. Celeste felt very comfortable in Italy. After their six months in Paris, Jean-Pierre had accepted a year's contract at the Palazzo Ducale. The Rijksmuseum in Amsterdam were already negotiating a contract with him after Venice. She enjoyed travelling with him, experiencing new countries and cultures. They would be in Italy for a full twelve months before returning back to England and then hopefully to The Netherlands.

Francois smiled and waved from the pram. "Lui...."

Walking along the Riva Del Ferro, she could hear the yellow and white vaporetti, chugging their way down the canal, pausing near the water stop, grinding to a halt and blustering like a mechanical dinosaur with an intestinal condition. A rope secured the boat to the dock. Passengers carefully left the rocking boat before another queue of people were allowed to embark.

Black and white, beautifully ornate gondolas seemed to slice through the water as they glided along the canal. The gondoliers all looked tall and strong as they assertively, placed their long oars into the water, which pushed the boats forward with a smooth and decisive ride.

Pausing at a nearby Tabacchi, she bought a bottle of chilled mineral water then walked towards Rialto Bridge. The area was busy with tourists taking photographs and buying souvenirs. Venice was always crowded, it was never a quiet time. She looked at the bridge and was not happy about carrying the pram and Francois. Although the journey should only have taken less than five minutes, the reality was she had to allow at least fifteen. Carefully adjusting his hat and ensuring his little face was covered with sun cream, she strapped him to her chest in a harness, folded the pram and started to climb the steps over the bridge, down the other side and towards the Rialto Mercato.

Crowded but exciting, she picked up her fresh fruit and vegetables, found a little coffee shop so they could enjoy a short rest, an espresso, her favourite chocolate croissant decorated with flaked almonds and a generous sprinkling of icing sugar. Francois drank his water and nibbled on a rusk biscuit. It melted on his fingers and he wiped it over his face. Extending his tongue to lick the food off, he looked messy but adorable. She cleaned him up with a wet wipe and then they left. After five minutes, it felt so hot that she decided to look for a bench where she could sit and relax with Francois.

Francois was quiet in his pram. He looked content as he played with his little toy car. Pulling the string, it made a sound. It always made him smile as if it was the first time he had heard the noise. Pulling it again and again: *Zoom-Zoom.* He was such a happy child and despite him being relaxed and comfortable, Celeste couldn't resist taking him out of the pram; she loved to hold him. He struggled as she put her hands around his small body and as she lifted him out, his little legs dangled in the air; in one swift movement he was nestled comfortably on her lap.

Looking up at Celeste, he smiled: "Zoom-Zoom mama". But the sunlight was in his eyes and he squirmed and squinted. Returned his gaze to the toy, he pulled the handle again.

"Yes my little sweetheart." She smiled at him. Such peaceful paradise, beautiful sunshine, savouring the fulfilment a mother enjoys with her child. She felt as if every aspect of her femininity was absolutely satisfied and filled with love. Jean-Pierre was so handsome and intelligent, he was the perfect man. She loved the way his mind worked; how his strategies and approaches would dissect the root of any problem within an instant. How he could see through the peripheral haze that sometimes blurred people's comprehension of an issue. How as he glanced through the contract for their apartment, despite the contract being almost fifteen pages, he immediately read the one line regarding the termination criteria which would have made them vulnerable in the event of an unscrupulous landlord. He always knew what to look for, the weakness, the pivotal point that always made the difference.

His focus and determination so strong and powerful, he sometimes would not listen to any alternative. Perhaps that was why he was so successful. His inner energies manifested themselves into realities, seemingly effortless. But for Jean-Pierre, it was to be expected and he sometimes failed to appreciate his luck and good fortune. Caring, loving, gentle but strong. Jean-Pierre she thought. Even just thinking his name made her feel good. She closed her eyes – thinking about him brought him back in an instant.

"I love your papa," she said to Francois.

"Papa" Francois repeated.

"Yes Francois. Papa. I love your papa so much. I'm nothing without him."

"Papa" he repeated. "Papa" – then he pulled the handle again and giggled as he watched the string slowly creep back into the toy car as it made its familiar sound.

Sitting in one of the most beautiful cities in the world, did it really ever get any better than this? Did she have absolutely everything she had ever wanted, dreamt about and aspired to during her transition from child to woman? The answer was a definite yes. Her world was full of so much happiness, almost beyond expression in its consuming sense of completion. If only her family had known Francois and met Jean-Pierre.

Putting Francois back into his pram, he resisted again. He preferred her lap and be began to cry. She took out some drink from her bag and handed him the bottle. He took it, drank and was happy again. It was getting even hotter and she needed to get before they were too tired.

Her pram laden with food, she started the walk back but stopped at a supermarket to pick up some cheese. She didn't know what time Jean-Pierre would be returning home that evening, so she would prepare something in advance then keep it cold in the fridge. If Jean-Pierre was late and returned after Francois' bedtime, they could have a quiet dinner on their own with a good bottle of Italian prosecco to savour with the food. A cool shower, perhaps together, then bed. She smiled at the potential celestial delights in her husband's arms.

She thought of Portia; they hadn't corresponded in a while. Was she happy? She only ever talked about Max and their outstanding love-life that only got better. Celeste instinctively knew Portia wasn't happy. When Portia was genuinely content, she didn't need to tell the world. Celeste wondered about her but not for too long. She never forgave her for that first night with Max.

Her life in Hampstead seemed like a lifetime ago, despite it only being a few years. After her parents had been killed in the car crash, there didn't seem to be anybody for her in England. Portia wrapped up with Max, no parents. She was alone and except for a few friends, it all felt so meaningless.

Portia had repeatedly promised to visit her but then there were excuses, problems with dates and now after all this time, it was embarrassing to suggest more options. Even if she did visit, where would she stay in their apartment? It just about accommodated her, Jean-Pierre and Francois. Portia would frown at its compact dimensions. She preferred five star hotels, bathrooms with bidets and room service. Would Portia visit her? See her baby? Meet her husband again? Celeste tried to be optimistic but knew it was unlikely. It was a difficult situation with Max despite the fact they had developed a relationship and seemingly, were very happy together.

For a few moments, Celeste felt strangely alone and missed the camaraderie she had enjoyed for so many years with her dearest friend. She never thought it would be like this; perhaps their promises and childlike fantasies were never destined to reach fruition. The odd email, there had been a Christmas greeting, card and present when Francois was born; the promise of an imminent visit.

"Come on Francois. Let's get our shopping and go home. But first, I think you've got a nappy full of present for me. You're a smelly little baby."

"Zoom-zoom" he giggled.

"Yes, we're zooming off that nappy and cleaning you up."

"Zoom mama" and he dropped the car into the pram as she took him out and put him on her knee.

"You know I loved you from the minute I first saw you." Celeste planted a tender kiss on Jean-Pierre's cheek. Francois was asleep in his cot, it was late and they were tired.

"Well if I make you feel like this, I consider myself a very lucky man." His smile was so incredibly sexy. Not a full smile but a half smile; he would tilt his head in a certain way and always, she felt immediately ready for sex. Lifting the wine glass to her mouth, she took a sip, then seductively licked her lips. They stared into each other's eyes. The magnetism between them, still tangible and electric.

The wine was cool and fresh, the evening was still warm but more comfortable than the day's sweltering sunshine. Jean-Pierre scooped up a large slice of mozzarella cheese with some focaccia and some salad. He liked how Celeste warmed up the bread, drizzled over olive oil then finished with a sprinkling of coarse sea-salt. Watching her prepare it gave him pleasure; he wasn't used to seeing a woman lovingly prepare him a meal. She enjoying cooking bread and had become quite an expert. The focaccia she made was infinitely better than anything bought in a shop. Simple food but tasty and satisfying. "There's more in the fridge" she teased looking at the large amount of food balanced on his bread.

"I know. I checked the fridge when I smelt home-cooking." He smiled and touched her shoulder. "I love you Celeste. So very deeply."

"When I saw you in that shop in Hampstead, I fell in love with you the moment I saw you. But you've never told me you felt the same. Not that it matters."

"Well it must 'matter' as you've mentioned it." Jean-Pierre smiled: "Except I didn't like your silly friend or that pretentious trouble maker on her arm." He thought about Portia and how he had felt. He was relieved she had never visited them. Over time he had fallen in love with Celeste and from the stories about Portia, knew he had married the right woman. Her friend was now irrelevant history.

"You know how I feel about Max… and why! But Portia and I have shared history. I do miss her. There really was so much more to her; she was just insecure."

"Do you still hear from her?" he asked with concern. Celeste was beginning to talk about her with renewed affection. "Why did you go to the gallery on that day?" He asked. "I've often wondered."

"Max wanted to go. Something about his father's work in Munich. I don't know the details. Jewellery doesn't interest me. Luckily for you…"

"What happened?"

"I don't know. Portia said something I wasn't listening. I can't remember much other than how the evening progressed and ended."

"Could that be because he was taking your friend?"

"No, not at all" Celeste denied but had to consider his point for a moment. She felt instantly guilty. "I don't like Max. I don't care about his problems. I didn't take too much notice."

"So this is how we meet. You look irresistibly beautiful and within a few minutes, our destinies are sealed." Jean-Pierre refilled their glasses with wine. "A chance meeting which changed my life. Funny how you can know in an instant when something's right." He didn't sound convincing but Celeste thought he was probably tired.

She stood up, bent over the table and kissed his forehead. As she reached over he noticed her blouse was undone rather more than usual. Extending his hand, he caressed her breast. She breathed deeply in response to his touch. Then she pulled away and sat back in the chair. "You looked so handsome. I love you so much Jean-Pierre. And our beautiful son. Every day I am grateful for what I have. What we have together and here in Venice. I love it that you travel for your work and can take us with you to the most wonderful places."

"I love it that you can come and share it with me."

"Will our honeymoon last forever?" She stared into his eyes with an expression so full of love and joy, her gentle disposition made him feel even manlier.

"Not if I can help it Celeste. You've shown me more happiness than I could ever have imagined. You've given me love and a family."

Jean-Pierre finished his mouthful of food, drank his wine, then he kissed her tenderly. Their mouths slightly parted, he opened hers with his tongue and probed inside. Gently holding her breast, he felt her body respond to his gentle and erotic embrace. With his other hand, he undid her blouse then pulled it open exposing her bra.

Moving his hand onto her lap, then deftly along the length of her skirt... under it and inside her panties. Teasingly he stroked her thigh, then inside her panties... then back to her thigh. Sensually teasing her, he gauged her responses so she would be excited, warm and ready; that she should savour the ultimate physical release from an erotically developed orgasm. Wandering, exploratory fingers touched her inner thighs as she parted her legs. His fingers now inside her panties, he touched her mound, curled her pubic hair around his fingers, then parted the gentle, warm and moist area, he pressed inside of her. Celeste moaned gently, then slightly tensed. Touching her deeply, he massaged her most sensitive parts until they hardened on his finger tip, he felt it shudder and a delicate pulse as her orgasm rose into full blossom.

Bending down, he put his head under her skirt and nestled his head between her thighs. Gently his tongue licked around her opening then in collusion with his finger; massaging and sucking this focal point of her passion, her moans became more intense. She tried to be quiet in case she woke Francois. Clutching the arms of the chair, she held tightly as she orgasmed, feeling the pulsations and rhythms of her response to his sensual manipulation. Her passionate response took her to wonderful, euphoric heights; Jean-Pierre enjoyed pleasing her.

"I never had multiple orgasms until you."

"And we're not finished yet my darling."

Standing up, he took her off the chair and carried her into the bedroom. He laid her on the bed then sensually undressed her. She removed his shirt and kissed his chest, lowered her head and excited him with her mouth. "Stop or it'll be over too quick."

He lay on his back and she straddled herself on top of him; gently lowering herself onto his penis, he felt hard and delightful. She tossed her head back then swayed and moved passionately and vigorously until she felt him lunge upwards in a mighty crescendo of passion. They kissed passionately as she gently lifted herself up and then lay beside him. They slept soundly in each other's arms; both immensely satisfied, content and very much in love.

Francois was crying. Jean-Pierre checked the clock: 3.13 a.m. Celeste was in a deep sleep. He got up, rubbed his slightly bloodshot brown eyes and ran his fingers through his thick black hair. Putting on some boxer shorts, he went into Francois's room. Francois had been very sick and had diarrhoea which had not been contained in the nappy; he was very flushed and hot.

Picking up the infant, Francois felt limp and sweaty, so Jean-Pierre took him to the bathroom, cleaned up his bottom and ran a tepid bath to clean him properly, to soothe him and make him comfortable. Francois was whimpering and not his usual bouncy self. Quickly and efficiently, he dried him, put some cream on his nappy rash then gave him a cool drink. Francois didn't want to drink it but Jean-Pierre was patient and picked up his little toy car for him to play with and to distract his attention whilst Jean-Pierre ensured that his son took regular sips of the water.

"Zoom" Francois said quietly.

"Zoom little man" Jean-Pierre replied, smiling at him. But then Francois was sick again, down his front, on the toy, onto Jean-Pierre's chest and also on the floor. As his vomit projectiled, Jean-Pierre was shocked at the volume and velocity. Now rather more alarmed, he washed and changed him again. Wiped himself down with a towel and cleaned the floor. Changing the sheets on the cot whilst Francois sat on the floor, he wondered whether he should wake Celeste. It was now 3.45 a.m. He peeked inside the bedroom; she looked so peaceful. Perhaps Francois would be OK now. But Francois was even redder and looked very tired. Whimpering and confused, he threw his toy away from him, then cried for it. Pointing to it, distressed: "Zoom".

Jean-Pierre washed and disinfected the toy and gave it back. He added some special minerals and salts to the water so Francois wouldn't dehydrate. Again, he encouraged him to drink. Francois pushed the bottle away, then cried for the toy. Carrying him into the bedroom, Jean-Pierre gently climbed back into bed and lay Francois between him and Celeste.

"Celeste," he whispered. "Francois's in bed with us. He's not well."

"Sure OK, night night" and she turned over.

"Celeste did you hear me?"

"Yes, yes, you're in the bed with us..." but then Francois started to cry again and Celeste woke up.

"What's wrong with Francois, he's on fire?"

"He's had diarrhoea and been sick. I dealt with it but didn't want to leave him in the bed on his own. Shall we call a doctor or take him to hospital?"

"Have you given him some Calpol to calm down his temperature?" Then she got out of bed and put on a nightshirt.

"No – I wasn't sure what to do. He's drinking a little bit but not much." He whispered gently, so as not to alarm Celeste before she woke up properly. He was very worried.

"Let's see if we can get his temperature down. If we take him out now, that would not be good for him either. Let's try and keep him comfortable another half an hour. If his temperature goes up, even slightly, we'll go straight to the hospital. Agreed?"

Going into the kitchen, Celeste got the temperature scanner and laid it on Francois's forehead. His temperature was 103° F. She gave him some Calpol, some more cooled water, put a damp cloth on his forehead then laid him back in the bed. They both took care of him, ensuring he regularly drank cooled water and was soothed with a damp, cold cloth. At 6.45 a.m. his fever broke and Francois had a healthy temperature.

Jean-Pierre brought Francois's cot in the room, changed his nappy again, applied a thick dollop of cream on his nappy rash and some talcum powder to make him comfortable; then the family slept soundly until 10 a.m. when Francois woke them up because he was hungry, and because his car had been dropped outside of the cot.

"Mama. Papa." Then holding onto the cot's bars, he started to jump up and down.

Friday was always busy; preparing the weekend's meals plus washing and cleaning-up the apartment. Celeste enjoyed her domestic routine but soon she would be returning back to work as a primary school teacher. She had found a part-time job nearby and it would only be for a few hours every day. Being with other children would be hard as she wouldn't be with her son. She thought of Portia who would never have these problems. She would marry her millionaire and kiss good-bye any thoughts of work. But then Celeste stopped – would she swap Jean-Pierre or Francois for anybody or anything? Absolutely not.

"Come on Francois, let's get ready and get to the shops. Plus a really strong espresso and some biscotti will wake me up. Or in your case, some rusks and a juice." He started to giggle and waved his little chubby arms up and down. She hugged him and held him tight.

"I love you Francois. I love you so much." He struggled within her tight embrace so she put him on the floor. He sat up and started flapping his arms again. "And where are your socks? Those cute little blue ones with the teddies?" Then she smiled. Would have surprised her if he had answered! She just liked talking to him, engaging with him, encouraging him to speak. One day he'd reply. One day he would be able to tell her. She couldn't wait until he spoke, until she knew more about his personality, what he was thinking, what he wanted, what he liked and how he felt. But until then, she would have to rely upon smiles, odd words, his tears and her instinct in order to gauge his feelings and deeds.

"What are you doing Jean-Pierre?" she called out from the bedroom. Yet again, another sleepless night with Jean-Pierre on the computer. He was always up late at night, searching, researching, emailing people, what was he up to? She wondered if perhaps he was talking to other women, he was so secretive.

"Jean-Pierre. Come back to bed. I want you."

"Not now Celeste. I'm busy." The lamp shining on the screen, Jean-Pierre was slumped in front of the computer, looked tired and weary. His small pile of paper and red folder by the side getting bigger by the day. Sometimes she heard his printer, chugging out paper at 4 a.m. But at least if Francois woke up early he would look after him.

"Come on. This was a long time ago. What's your fascination with this? If you want misery, do the housework, washing and make breakfast." She walked over to him, massaged his shoulders and kissed the top of his head. She noticed that his hair was getting a little bit thin on top. She smiled and kissed the wannabe patch… Her dear handsome Jean-Pierre, going bald. She imagined him with a bald head. He would still be handsome. She imagined him putting on weight and looking middle-aged. She would still love him. In fact, there was nothing in the world that would ever stop her loving him.

"Please Celeste. Not now." She felt rejected but moved away.

"You're in a bad mood," she teased. "Some fresh orange juice. I'm going to have some."

"Go back to bed Celeste. It's 2 a.m."

"Just making sure you weren't chatting up other women… Women gagging for it."

"What's this 'gagging'. What's this word, I don't know it."

"It doesn't matter," she laughed.

"Please Celeste. What's this silly word 'gagging'."

"It means desperate. Are you looking for women who are desperate to be
made love to."

"Look at my piles of paperwork and research. You're being childish. You're too good for this Celeste. Please…." Then he paused, seeing her face was slightly hurt. "You mean there would be this amount of women 'gaggling'…"

"Gagging. Jean-Pierre . There isn't an l in Gagging. They're not geese as in gaggle of geese."

"OK – gagging – women gagging for it. Are you gagging for it?" Although not in the mood to play, he realized he had been a bit too sharp with her. He was in the wrong, it wasn't fair to vent at her. She was just trying to lighten his mood.

"Well I might have been, but you're clearly not in the frame of mind. So I'll gag away and gag alone…"

"Give me just another ten minutes and I'll sort out your 'gagging'. But a nice fresh orange juice would be nice too. And perhaps a croissant. You know the ones I like. With the almond paste in the middle."

She squeezed the oranges and put a croissant on his plate then went back to bed. Ten minutes later and she could hear he was still tapping away. Twenty minutes later he was making notes. Half an hour later, she turned off her light and went back to sleep.

When her alarm went off at 6.30 a.m. Jean-Pierre was not beside her. Francois had started to cry for his breakfast. Startled, she got out of bed and went into the living room. Jean-Pierre was still working, oblivious of the time and his surroundings.

"Jean-Pierre – what is this?"

"No Celeste. Please, just give me another ten minutes then I'll come back to bed."

He had made more posts on the internet and had even built his own website with research so far. But Celeste had no interest and never looked at the website. Whatever this interest, it took his time away from her and Francois. She was bored if he even mentioned this stupid obsession with old jewellery. She sometimes felt as if she competed for his time with another love interest.

But the website was now live, he was looking for anybody who knew something or anything about a certain piece of jewellery. He wanted to talk about it but knew she was bored. Portia had worn her out with endless conversations about the past, so rather than continue a similar theme with Jean-Pierre, it was simply a no-go area. He understood and never elaborated. This was his fight not hers.

"Can you hear Francois crying?" Celeste shouted from the bedroom.

"Sorry, sorry, sorry." He got out of the chair and into Francois's room, picked him out of the cot and took him into the kitchen where he warmed up some milk for him.

"Cup of your favourite espresso Celeste?"

"No Jean-Pierre. Don't worry. I'll help myself."

She walked over to the piles of paperwork, glancing through the material that kept him up all night. The research, notes and endless surfing for information that seemed to have obsessed him for the last few months.

She didn't hear him walk back into the room. "Celeste, what are you doing?"

"Looking at this. Will you not find any peace until you have your answers? You have us Jean-Pierre, me and Francois. Isn't that enough? I respect and love you." She kissed him then took Francois out of his arms, back into the kitchen and for his breakfast. Putting on the coffee machine, she brought Jean-Pierre in a fresh, black Americano which he eagerly accepted and drank.

"Wasn't there an orange juice?"

Celeste pointed to it at the corner of the table. Untouched and with the orange bits still floating on the top. "Not-so-fresh. Want another one?"

"No it's all right. I'm nearly done. I'll grab a quick hot shower and go to the gallery."

"You haven't slept. You must be exhausted."

"I am – but I'll leave this for a little while. We'll have a nice evening together later. Just the three of us." He kissed her on the cheek, then went into the kitchen and kissed Francois. Then he remembered his own childhood…

"What's wrong JP? You look deep in thought. Are you worried about something?" Celeste asked with loving concern.

"Just thinking about my family."

"We are your family."

"You know what I mean. Where Francois fit in with the family thread. What is he extending? Were they good people; were they bad people?"

"I doubt if they were bad. Look at you and Francois. You're perfection!" she teased. "You think too much. Francois is yours and he's mine. I had enough confusion with parentage from my friendship with Portia. I live for the day and accept what I know. Your father loved you and it's his choice if he didn't want to talk about his past."

"I still needs answers."

" Am I the only person who's happy with what they know? It's no big deal. Leave it where it is… history! Call me Bubbles after

Michael Jackson's monkey and I'd be fine. I'm happy with who and what I am. Nothing else matters."

Celeste noticed he was clearly worried about something and had stopped listening to her. Whatever was bothering him would be discussed when he was ready. For now, he was deep in thought and carefully treading his way through a turmoil of emotions and inner conflicts.

Jean-Pierre thought about his childhood home. His French mother was beautiful; his father loved her and never got over the betrayal and divorce. It had affected him terribly. He often talked about rejection. If his mother could betray him and his father, how could he ever trust a woman? But then there was Celeste. She had followed him everywhere never queried or argued. She had been alone but had found comfort with him and their family. She brought out aspects of his personality that no other woman had touched. She was special. He couldn't imagine his life without her and didn't even want to ponder that thought for a moment. He loved her. They had found a balance, love and a companionship which developed into a marital and committed, beautiful relationship. And now with a blessed son that made their union complete.

Looking at his paperwork, he wanted to find the truth about his grandparents. Who they were, what they did? Why they sent their child, his father to England without them? More importantly, what was the connection with the panther brooch? For years he had visited galleries and every exhibition themed with animal jewellery.

So far this endeavour had only led to his success at meeting Celeste. Perhaps that was his destiny. Perhaps this was the only point.

He looked at the Prague file and an etching of the two brooches: A panther and snake; both had diamond eyes. A single sheet of paper with just one word: Sarah. Would it be possible to ever piece it all together? There just wasn't enough clues for it all to make sense. The only person onside to support his endeavour was Mr. Kauff from the gallery in Knightsbridge. He also had a picture on his website of the two brooches and a direct contact number and email for anybody who might know about their origins or owners; or of the secrets that surrounded these pieces. All art houses that exhibited jewelled animals had been approached, yet despite its international and vigorous promotion, there was never any response or hint at further clues. Perhaps the people who knew the story were dead.

He heard Celeste get out of bed so he shut off his computer. Put the picture and blank sheets back in the Prague box and locked it. There shouldn't be secrets between a husband and wife but Celeste had accepted his mission. If anything she had been sympathetic because of her friendship with Portia. She never asked questions and was happy to take him for what and he was; her husband and father of their child.

Jean-Pierre walked into Francois's room and watched his son sleep. So peaceful in his ignorance of what life was about. As long as he had his parents, his food and somewhere safe to sleep and play, his baby years should be treasured. Only so long before the realities and confusion of adulthood swamp what is so easily taken for granted. What would he tell his son when he asked about his background? He couldn't imagine for one moment that Celeste would find another husband and lose interest in Francois. He was her life, her *raison d'etre*. It was also part of what made her so beautiful, simply because she personified love to all those she held close and dear.

Jean-Pierre packed his suitcase, his trip to the Metropolitan Museum of Art in New York had been brought forward. Originally just for a week, they were now setting-up meetings which necessitated him going for ten days. She entered the room holding three ironed shirts.

"I need you. Francois needs you. New York needs you. We all take our turn." She smiled sexily, stroked his shoulder than tapped his chest. "For how long?"

"I'm not sure. At worst two weeks. Will you be OK here without me?"

"I'll survive. Perhaps I'll find another man to keep me warm at night" she teased.

"I'd never leave you for a second if I thought that was a possibility."

"And you have all those sexy young Manhattan girls. The Sex in the City types."

"You insecure woman." He bent over and kissed her on the lips. Gently then more passionately as the physical dynamism of their love and tenderness consumed them both in an intimate embrace. "I take after my father, not my mother! But seriously Celeste, maybe somebody should stay with you to keep you company?"

"Perhaps" and she thought of Portia. "I know you don't like her but if you're not here... it's been a long time and time heals wounds and rifts. We were close friends and I miss her. Also I'd like her to get to know Francois. Would you mind?"

"You don't need to ask Celeste. This is your home too. But I remember Portia, no men here" he teased. "And especially that boyfriend of hers."

"Don't worry – just girl-time – me and Portia. I've had quite a few emails from her. I'm sending one-liners but I miss her." Jean-Pierre noticed she looked sad and clearly needed her friend. "I had an email from her last week, she's not happy. Something's wrong. I'm not sure what's happening between her and Max. When I see her, she'll tell me more. I'd like to invite her to stay with us. Time does heal and we grew up together. We have a lot of history."

"It's hardly surprising she has a problem with Max. The man's a pig."

"Ahhh – you're biased" she soothed. "He can't be THAT bad if Portia's in love with him. I know some of the men she's dated... And despite her flaws – there's a sensitivity there. For her, sex is affection. Even though she doesn't understand it herself. Maybe now she's grown up. I'd like to give her the benefit of the doubt."

"Don't tell me about her. I'll probably dislike her even more. But your home – your friend. Wait for me to go though. And then you two, or rather three with Francois, have fun. Francois can be your chaperone. He's the man of the house now!"

That evening, Celeste replied to Portia's email.

Hi Portia.

How are you and Max?

Sorry not been in touch for a while. Been busy here and Francois takes up so much of my time. But I love him dearly and perhaps it would be good for us to meet up.

Jean-Pierre is away for a few weeks in New York. Care to take an impromptu trip to Venice?

Celeste and Francois x

P.S. Don't bring Max.

"Portia" Celeste called out excitedly from behind the barrier in the Arrivals section of Marco Polo airport. Francois started to wave and was laughing. If his mother was excited – so was he. "Portia" she called again. This time Portia saw them and waved back.

"WOW. WOW. WOW" she said looking at Francois. "Please, please let me hold him." Celeste passed Francois to him then kissed Portia on the cheek then the three embraced warmly. "You are so lucky Celeste. You are so lucky. And I'm lucky to be here with you. Thank You – thank you for inviting me to spend some time with your family."

"Enough time has passed Portia."

"More than enough. Come, let's not be all emotional, let's be happy. Let's celebrate our reunion and your handsome little boy. Oh Celeste – I'm so glad to see you. I'm so glad to be here."

"Big problems?" Celeste asked. Portia was just too happy… to be happy.

"How long have you got? At least I'm here with you. I've missed you. I've needed you. More than I could have ever imagined." She hugged Francois who put his little hands on her shoulders.

"Zoom" and they all laughed.

"Come on Portia. Let's get the transfer into Venice and then we can sit somewhere quiet and talk properly."

Portia sat with Francois on her lap. He was adorable. So well-behaved and happy.

"It's not surprising you would have such a wonderful child Celeste. You were always a mother-in-waiting. Not like me. I'd be terrible."

"No you wouldn't. You don't know what you're capable of until it happens. Honestly Portia, you'd be great."

"How can you tell that?"

"Because you're capable of love. And essentially, that's what it takes to be a mother. But first, imagine loving somebody more than yourself."

"That wouldn't be hard." She cuddled Francois close. He seemed comfortable with her and nestled snuggly onto her chest.

"You've grown-up Portia. You really have." Portia nodded unable to speak. Holding Francois close she regretted the time that had passed. She had already missed so much. She should never be parted from Celeste for so long. Especially now.

Exiting the bus station at Pizzale le Roma, they walked towards the nearest vaporetto station. Portia looked along the Grand Canal and took in a deep, theatrical breath. Venice's pulse and vibrancy made it irresistible and seductive. "I love it here Celeste. I absolutely love it."

Within a few minutes, the Linea 1 vaporetto arrived and Celeste struggled to get Francois and his pram onto the boat. Portia and a strange man helped her.

"I bet you can't wait until Francois can walk?" Portia teased.

"I've been trying to teach him since before he could crawl" and those around them who understood English chuckled to themselves.

Portia hadn't been to Venice for years and was fascinated: "I had almost forgotten how pretty, I mean beautiful it is here."

"How could you forget? Only problem is that it's not particularly child friendly for prams and heavy shopping." Within just a few minutes they arrived to their destination. Celeste waited for the boat to stop rocking before she made her way to the exit. Portia paused to take in the air and smell, she wanted to drag Venice deep into her soul and then nourish her body with its every nuance.

The area was full of tourists, speaking a full array of languages, the noise an inaudible sound of international linguistics and accents. The wheels from their suitcases rattled along the paving stones and clanked down the stairs as they were dragged. Portia looked at the women and felt aware she was probably the only one in a skirt. The women were predominantly wearing trousers which were probably due to the practicality of travelling in Venice rather than a sense of style or fashion. Between all the steps and hopping on and off the vaporetti, a skirt would be awkward and potentially too revealing.

When they arrived back to the apartment, Jean-Pierre had received a letter from Prague. The addressee was a Veronika Kubiskla. She put it on his bedside cabinet. She meant to text him about the letter in case he wanted her to open it. But she didn't and then she forgot. He was always getting letters from around the world and most were charities asking him to support them on a voluntary basis. He didn't need to give away any more of his time. She and Francois needed him.

Portia spoke for over an hour, barely pausing for breath as she went into detail about her relationship with Max, the trip to Prague, the dark shadows. Celeste was deeply shocked by Portia's story; it was incredible and despite Portia's tendency to elaborate to the point of excessive poetic licence, even at its minimal, her story was worrying. She could never tell Jean-Pierre all the details. He barely tolerated Portia anyway, this would have confirmed his worst suspicions.

They sat in the small lounge area. A few comfortable chairs, some large original paintings by local Italian artists hung on the walls. Stacks of books, an old wooden table that doubled up as Jean-Pierre's desk. Francois's high-chair in the corner, his toys in a tidy box. Celeste knew that Portia would not have approved the décor, it was comfortable and practical as compared to Portia's sense of extravagant. A stone floor with a slightly worn rug in its centre. Portia wondered if Celeste had noticed the small hole in the corner where a guest had dropped a cigarette.

"What are you thinking Portia?" Celeste asked her.

Portia was looking at the floor, a tissue held to her nose. "Everything and nothing. The waste of time. The relationship. What I had hoped for and the nightmare that was Prague. At night I sometimes sense those shadows. I'm scared to sleep. I'm too frightened to close my eyes." Francois started to cry too sensing her unhappiness.

"Please Portia. Francois's crying too." Portia forced a smile, if only to soothe the child.

"A beautiful child, a loving husband. You have everything."

"To you I have everything?" She laughed and startled Francois. He started to cry again.

"Please Celeste. May I hold him?"

Portia sat comfortably and Celeste placed him on her lap. He had stopped crying but wasn't absolutely happy being on Portia's lap rather than his mother's. He kept looking at Celeste for reassurance that he was safe. He would accept Portia's lap, just as long as Celeste was still in the room and visible. As the child began to relax, Portia held him closer and then gently she cradled him. He didn't fight her but looked over her shoulder for Celeste. She was still there. He was content. And then he relaxed again.

"You're gorgeous Francois" Portia whispered. "So perfect. Probably the only perfect man on this planet."

"Come on Portia. Don't be like that. OK – I'm biased Francois is perfect but he's not the only man who is," and they smiled. Francois smiled too. He started to stroke Portia's face, his big brown eyes wide and alert. When he smiled, he had little dimples in his cheeks and he dribbled. Portia picked up a tissue and wiped his mouth.

"I mean it Celeste. You have everything."

"My home wouldn't live up to your expectations. I know you Portia – probably too well. You'd never settle for a shabby rug and past its sell-by-date furniture."

"Perhaps not a few years ago and I know I was perhaps… a tad materialistic."

"Tad. How about absolutely…"

"Potentially," she conceded. "But you have happiness, a wonderful family, something of purpose. I have nothing Celeste. Nothing worth anything."

"Stop wallowing, you're getting depressing. Hug my son whilst I prepare some light supper. Are you hungry?" She went into the kitchen and took out some pasta, parmesan, basil, fresh and plump beef tomatoes and a large bottle of garlic infused olive oil. Wondering whether to cook some pasta, she waited for Portia's reply.

"As long as I can cuddle and hug your son, I'll eat anything."

Putting Francois on the floor, he crawled around and picked up some toy soldiers and then his favourite car. Portia got on the floor too and played with him.

He chuckled and laughed: "Zoom zoom" he said.

"Zoom zoom Francois. And I bet you have a wonderful car when you grow up." She lightly kissed the top of his head. He looked up and smiled, his chubby little fingers clutching the car. He held it up to her, gesturing her to take it in order to play with him. At that moment, for that split second, this little innocent gesture was the best gift she could ever have. She thought of the hands that offered her jewellery. The hands that explored her caressed her; the hands that made her feel soiled and cheap. Then this little babyish hand, holding the little red toy car so she should play with him. His most prized possession. Sharing his game, wanting to play, inviting her into his world of make believe and pretend.

"Zoom Francois." Then the tears flowed and she couldn't stop them. Francois put down the car and put his arms up to her. She picked him up, sat in the chair and held him tightly. He didn't move, squirm or cry. He just outstretched his arms as wide as he could. Innocent eyes that seemed to have a depth of understanding. Francois understood that when you're sad, you need to be held close so you feel safe.

"Can I borrow your laptop?" Portia asked Celeste.

"Sure and she handed her the computer.

"It's just that I haven't checked my emails for days and just wondering if…"

"If Max has tried to contact you?"

Portia sat pensively. Celeste just raised her eyebrows. "Perhaps. I'm not sure if I want to hear from him or not. In some respects I want to move away from him. Everything I've said to you, it's all so awful but then… I don't know. I just wonder. Wonder if?"

"So check your emails and see. Then you'll know and can decide from there."

Celeste entered her password, turned the computer around, then picked up Francois and took him into her bedroom.

Nervously Celeste logged in. She had ten emails, seven were from Max.

To: Portia D'Allegro
From: Maximilian Schultzmann
I don't know what's happened. Where are u?
Max

To: Portia D'Allegro
From: Maximilian Schultzmann
Portia. Don't ignore me. Email me back. Max x"

To: Portia D'Allegro
From: Maximilian Schultzmann
Subject: US

WHERE ARE U? WHY DONT YOU REPLY?????????????????????

To: Portia D'Allegro

From: Maximilian Schultzmann

Subject: US

Is this it?

To: Portia D'Allegro

From: Maximilian Schultzmann

Subject: US

Dont ignore me. I wont wait.

To: Portia D'Allegro

From: Maximilian Schultzmann

Subject:US

I'LL MISS YOU. BYE

Max

To: Portia D'Allegro

From: Maximilian Schultzmann

Subject: Us

Am resending in case you didnt get emails.

To: Maximilian Schultzmann

From: Portia D'Allegro

Subject:Reply from Portia to Max

Perhaps it's better that we decide to just go our own ways. I loved you very much. I don't understand what happened in Prague but now I need space. I need to put things into perspective. I'm in Venice with Celeste and Francois.

Portia.

She stared at the YOUR MESSAGE HAS BEEN SENT.
Two minutes later she received a reply.

From:Maximilian Schultzmann
To: Portia D'Allegro
Subject:Reply from Portia to Max
Gettin next plane. Love you.
Max

Should she tell him not to bother? Celeste and Jean-Pierre would not be pleased to see him; surely he would book a hotel and not expect to stay with them. Of course he would. Especially with Francois in the small apartment.

Then a flash as another email was received:

To: Portia D'Allegro
From: Maximilian Schultzmann
Subject:Reply from Portia to Max

Flight booked. Coming in 2 day. Will send confirm and itin. Wait for me at airport. Will come to Marco Polo via Alitalia. Meet me there.

Portia turned off the computer.

Celeste sat quietly as Portia told her of the email dialogue. "Are you angry?" she asked.

"No Portia. You must do what's right for you? You've been with him a long time. You want to make sure. It's understandable." Celeste's tone was one of boredom. Secretly she had hoped that Portia had split with Max. She disliked him intensely but it was Portia's decision. But under no circumstance, would Max be welcome at her home.

"Perhaps the four of us could go to dinner when Jean-Pierre's back?" Portia asked.

"Now, you're pushing it Portia. You do what you want with Max. It's none of my business. We've seen enough of him, we're not interested, we don't like him and we never have. But if you love him and want to make a life with him, that's your decision. If you married him I would go for old time's sake. But Portia. You've only been here a few days and already, it feels as if we 're back into a bad time."

"I can't help it I know you're right and I'm sorry. I don't know why I emailed him. I just felt that I should."

Celeste was quiet, their relationship had lost its consistency, but… the good and the happy times outweighed the problem areas. "I'd be there to see you married and would pray that whoever he was, would love you, care for you and make you as happy as JP makes me. I know what it is to be happy and in love. I want you to have the same."

Portia thought of Jean-Pierre and how he was the perfect father and son. How could Max possibly compare to him?

Chapter 6

Max called the taxi company for the third time in twenty minutes. Where was his taxi. Standing outside his flat, he looked anxiously for the familiar limousine. At last, he got through to the operator:

"Just where the fuck is the car?"

"On its way Mr. Schultzmann. It's been caught up in traffic but on its way."

"I should bloody hope so. I'm running late and do NOT want to miss my flight."

"I'll call the driver and check. Please hold." Three minutes later she came back online. "I'm sorry but the car has had a problem. A flat tyre. We're despatching another car now. Should be with you in twenty minutes."

"Twenty minutes. Just leave it. I'll get a black cab." He slammed the phone down and went back into his apartment block and yelled at the concierge. They called their regular taxi company. Nothing was available or within a five mile radius. So they called a local mini cab company. They too were busy. They called a black taxi company who confirmed it would be a thirty minute wait.

Max looked at his watch. His flight was due to depart in two and a half hours. He saw a passing taxi and hailed it. They were caught in traffic and arrived to the airport as the gate was closing. He then had to queue for another taxi to take him back to St John's Wood.

Portia sat alone outside a café in St. Marks Square. Celeste had taken Francois to a friend for the afternoon. Portia wanted to give her and Francois some time alone after their return.

Her table was directly across from the Campanile di San Marco and to her left, the imposing and majestic, white Basilica di San Marco. The hot chocolate was comforting and sipping it gave her a diversion from her own, internal thoughts. It was very thick and coated the inside of her mouth.

A pigeon landed on her table and seemed to defy her for being there; she felt as if she had encroached upon his turf! The pigeon just stared, walked about and pecked for crumbs on the table. As the drink was expensive due to the café's prime position, she was loathe to just get up and leave because of an uninvited guest. She decided to sit the pigeon out. After around a minute or so, the bird got the hint then flew away. Portia felt a mild sense of achievement.

She took another sip and looked around and wondered if she should be taking lots of photographs. She couldn't be bothered. Buying a guide book would have had better quality images and anyway, there was nobody to take a photograph which would have included her with an architectural highlight in the background. She drank some more chocolate then run her tongue around her mouth. She should have been there with Max. What on earth happened at the airport? Why did he miss the plane?

When he called her to explain there had been a problem, he blamed taxis and London in general. Between the lines of his argument, he just hadn't allowed enough time. His anger seemed controlled but she knew him better than to believe everything he said. It must have been terrible. He was probably angry and swearing. Erroneously thinking that if he shouted, he would get what he wanted. Feeling bored of sitting on her own, she paid the bill then headed off.

Walking down the Piazza San Marco, she approached the canal. It was busy and there was a long queue for gondolas. Who would want to get in that she thought? How tacky, how touristy… as she walked away she glanced back. An oriental middle-aged couple were scrambling to get in, trying to get cosy in the wooden seats. It was windy down the Grand Canal so they pulled a blanket over themselves to keep warm, then snuggled tightly together. They seemed very happy. The gondolier took a photograph of them.

As she walked past a bar, some Italian men spotted her and called out: "Buonasera bella." She ignored them. They said something else to her in Italian that she didn't understand. Pausing, she looked back and they waved. Should she? Shouldn't she? She did! The two men were friendly. Wearing short sleeve shirts and shorts, they were tanned, healthy looking and physically fit. They were drinking beer from the bottle. They were clearly linked to the bar but standing up against a wall near some street vendors selling souvenirs. They were both flirting. She flirted with them both too.

"So what brings you out on this beautiful evening? And why leave your boyfriend or husband at home alone."

"My BOYFRIEND is not here. Yet!"

"Silly man" the other man laughed. "By the way, my name is Giannini and my friend is Roberto.

"Excuse Giannini. He chatsa up all the bootiful women. And now we know that you are new, because, you would not 'av told us 'bout your boyfriend." Both men smiled and nudged each other.

"Perhaps. But please, for real, my boyfriend should have flown in today and was delayed. He will be here soon, probably tomorrow." She was feeling uncomfortable and thought how easy it would be to just keep walking; walking away from them.

"So you know our names. What is yours?"

She hesitated before replying: "Portia."

"Portia – nice name. Your family Italian? You are bootiful and have a bootiful Italian name. You must be Italian."

"No and hey – that was a bit quick. I'm here with a good friend and her son. I am staying at their apartment. I needed some time alone. I'm not looking for anything" she said purposefully. "So we can chat, or I can walk on." The two men got the hint and their camaraderie and over familiarity towards her cooled.

The evening felt refreshing, a breeze blew in from the canal. The freshness of the night air, the water, music, people laughing, relaxed, enjoying themselves. She closed her eyes for a few moments. It felt so peaceful.

"Ah, I think we are boring you" Roberto teased as he finished his bottle of Peroni. He put it on top of the wall then crossed his arms.

"No, not at all. Just taking in the atmosphere and everything. So relaxed. Being near water makes you calmer."

"Well I've never quite thought of it like that but I suppose so," Giannini replied pensively. "You seem so happy but at the same time, like something or perhaps, somebody is missing."

"That's personal. Alone but not lonely."

The three of them stood in silence. "Sorry and thank you for the chat but I really need to get going now. I'm tired. It's been a long day."

Giannini looked at Roberto who just nodded. A secret code between the two friends.

"You're a stranger here, let me walk you back to your friend's apartment. You don't want to be walking around alone." He seemed sincere and gentle despite the clichéd chat-up lines.

He put his mobile and keys into his pocket and mumbled something to his friend in Italian. Both men left without paying for their drinks. They just waved at another man who she assumed to be the owner.

"Come on Portia. Where does your friend live, can we walk there or should we get the vaporetto ?"

"She lives near the Rialto Bridge."

"So let's walk. We can go past the Chiesa di San Salvatore and straight through. Just one road" and he started walking.

"But I got the vaporetto here."

"No, long way 'round. Quick walk. No time. Come…" Giannini seemed so decisive and certain, she would have felt silly arguing with him. Perhaps he was right? Perhaps she shouldn't walk back alone.

They started walking down the road but then he hesitated to take a cigarette box out of his pocket. The road was dark but the flame from the lighter made a flattering shadow across his face as he lit a cigarette. She stared at him and found him extremely attractive. She looked back and smiled. Then he lent forward kissed her gently on the lips. She angrily stood back but as she pulled away a waft of his after shave filled her nostrils. It was very sexy. He smiled. As if he knew her thoughts.

"It was nothing."

"Cigarette?" he asked.

"I don't smoke" she replied.

He looked at the cigarette as if wondering whether he should extinguish. "Do you mind if I smoke?" he took it out of his mouth and held it as if ready to throw onto the floor.

"I don't mind. It's up to you. You're hardly going to be kissing me so why should I care?" she laughed.

"But I already have."

He slowly brought the cigarette to his mouth. He took a few breaths then threw it on the floor and rubbed his shoe on it to extinguish. He had that special sexual charisma which turned handsome men into film stars.

"I told you, I'm with someone" she said. She tried to sound convincing as if her relationship was in a non-negotiable scenario that was established and strong. She doubted whether her tone endorsed her intention. She sounded more like a school girl who pretended to have a boyfriend.

"Yes you said. But perhaps your eyes and body say something different." She noticed a scar on his left cheek too.

"What happened to your cheek?" she asked.

"War wound" he teased.

"You were attacked?" she asked with concern.

"No. I'm joking with you. A drunken evening and I fell over and cut my cheek." He touched the scar then shrugged his shoulders. "And my nose broke at the same time. Just in case you were wondering. But if you want me to be a hero, I can do that too! But I would prefer to be your lover." He winked and smiled. "And I am only teasing. Come on, let's get you back to your friend."

"Ever the charmer."

"You find me charming?" Portia felt warm towards him, despite his bravado he seemed vulnerable. They walked quickly and very soon, they were near Celeste's apartment. Portia was slightly disappointed that the cut through was so quick.

"My friend has an apartment over a flower shop." She pointed towards a shop approximately 100 yards down the road.

"Ah, so we're nearly there and our little walk will soon be over."

"Yes," she replied with a note of disappointment. "I'm grateful you walked me back. That was kind of you."

"You English are so formal. *I'm so grateful*" he teased with an English accent. "You need to relax a little, enjoy yourself. Let go. Do you ever let go?"

"Yes."

"Would you let go if I said I'd like to kiss you goodnight? Kiss you properly." Portia was surprised, this was quick but she wasn't entirely perturbed by the gesture either. He moved his face closer to hers.

"Aren't you being a bit forward?" she whispered but without wanting to deter him.

"Probably. But here we don't worry too much about these sorts of formalities. I'm a man and you're a very attractive woman. If I want to kiss you, I won't wait for three weeks before asking. We don't stand on ceremony but rather than just take, I'll ask you. Life's too short. So?.."

"I suppose...." But before she could finish her sentence, he held her face in his hands and started to kiss her. Gently at first, his mouth exploring her lips. When she tried to speak and opened her mouth, instead he used the parting as an entrance for his tongue to delve into her mouth. Kissing her passionately, his kiss was strong and manly. His arms held her tight, stroking her back. Wanting to resist, she also wanted to ardently respond. His kiss was forceful and more passionate than anything she had remembered with Max. She felt excited but she didn't feel guilty. She wanted some affection but nothing complicated. She felt lonely and unloved.

"Would your friend mind if I came up for a coffee?"

"YES SHE WOULD" Portia stated. "And no, you can't. That's really pushing the boundaries!"

He smiled, the left side of his lips more upturned than his right. "Well after a kiss like that, you can't blame me for asking. For an English girl, you've got a lot of passion."

"What do you mean *for an English girl,*" she said, mimicking his Italian accent.

"I think your boyfriend isn't looking after you as well as he should and that perhaps an Italian man might be better for you. You have beautiful green eyes." She wanted to be indignant and protective of Max. But she had hesitated too long for any response to be convincing.

"I need to go inside now. It's getting late and I'm tired."

"You are here, above this shop?"

"Yes."

"OK flower girl. Pick you up at seven o'clock tomorrow. Have you tried gnocchi?"

"I'm busy tomorrow."

"Yes you are. I'm taking you out for gnocchi." He bent over and kissed her on the cheek, turned around and walked away. As she stood there wondering if she had agreed to a date, she shook her head then called out. "Give me your number. I'm not sure I can make it." But there was no reply. He had gone, disappeared into the night air and the dark, back streets.

All she had was the feel and taste of his mouth on hers. The smell of his aftershave still teasing her nostrils. The feel of his body pressed close against hers. His expression which assumed a great deal, confident, manly and strong. She wanted to be angry but instead she felt intrigued and just slightly damp between her thighs.

Would he really be here to pick her up tomorrow or was he just pretending, lying to see if she would react? She didn't know whether to be excited at the thought of seeing him again or guilty that potentially, she would cheat on Max. She'd never cheated on Max. Max. Max. That night in Prague. With whatever happened at the airport he should have been in Italy with her. Instead he was in the UK blaming the world for everything rather than take responsibility for his actions. He was probably out with Andre, chasing women... she remembered the magazines. She shook her head trying to dispel the thought of him having sex with another woman. It wasn't too difficult to imagine. In fact it was too easy...

She saw the way Max would eye pretty women; waitresses in restaurants, girls in shops, girls passing him on the street. Any woman, any girl. Preferably, tall, slim and blonde. But short and brunette would do too! He made her feel inferior as if she was in competition with every woman he met. That she should remain perfect as he constantly compared. She had never thought about it before, probably because she was just too close but standing back, things looked different. Her relationship felt different. She never compared him to other men... until now. She now compared him to Jean-Pierre and Giannini.

It was 6 p.m. and Portia wondered whether to get ready or not. She had mentioned Giannini to Celeste, just in case he turned up but she pretended not to be too bothered. However she did shower, had bought a new summer dress and some designer Italian jewellery just in case he appeared. She didn't wear too much make-up, she noticed Italian girls were more natural. Concentrated on eyes and lips. It was the foreigners who wore too much make-up. It just so happened that she bought a new black kohl pencil to accentuate her green eyes.

At 7 p.m. he didn't turn up. At 7.15 p.m. he was still not there. At 7.30 p.m. she felt disappointed but laughed it off. Celeste and Portia sat in silence. Then the doorbell rang. He was over half-an-hour late. She wanted to be angry but Celeste intervened: "In Italy, we don't always run to time. We don't bother so much about these details, especially when we're relaxing." Celeste looked out of the window. He's nice looking Portia, behave yourself... If you must" and she smiled. "But not here, not with Francois in the flat!"

"I'm not like that now. I've grown up."

145

"Yes of course. But if he were my date – I'd be thinking about it." Portia looked out of the window too. He was standing on the pavement, smoking a cigarette. He was wearing an open necked white shirt and tight jeans. He turned around and saw them looking out of the window. "Nice. One beautiful woman would have been enough. But two is even better. Come on flower girl, we'll be late."

"Late" she shouted back. "You can talk!"

"I'm worth waiting for…"

Carefully Portia went downstairs, she was wearing heels which were noisy going down the metal staircase.

He greeted her with a gentle kiss and hug then looked her up and down. "Here we walk, I think that perhaps your shoes will be difficult. Do you have others? Come on, it's a lovely evening, change your shoes." He wasn't suggesting, he was telling her."

"But my shoes complement my dress."

"So what. You won't be comfortable in them. Be practical. It's a nice evening, we'll walk and get some supper." He put his arm around her and squeezed. "Just teasing you. That's for the next date!"

Reluctantly, she walked back up the metal staircase and got some sandals. She was wearing a red summer dress and her sandals were green. She felt like a Christmas tree. Celeste laughed. "Do I look ridiculous?"

"No" Giannini replied, standing in the doorway.

"Hello" he said to Celeste. "Nice place you have here."

"Come in, would you like something to drink? An espresso or something cold?" She felt compelled to invite him in but was not happy to see him standing in the doorway. He sensed her annoyance and didn't venture into the apartment but just stood by the door.

"No, I'm fine" he replied.

Portia was shocked that he had followed her up the stairs without invitation. Celeste sensed what Portia was thinking. Giannini and Celeste spoke in Italian then laughed and Portia noticed Celeste seemed to relax.

"Giannini, we must speak in English. We're being rude."

"I know. And Celeste, you picked that up quick. I can't believe you can already speak Italian."

"Not really. Just basics. A few months ago I was speaking French, soon I'll be speaking Dutch. Am trying, makes life easier although everybody always speaks English. Don't worry."

"Come on Portia, let's get that gnocchi."

"Have a good time you two," Celeste called as they walked out of the door.

"Ok. See you soon" Giannini replied.

They ate, laughed and enjoyed the food and wine. Portia had drunk too much prosecco and felt giddy and light-headed. As they walked away from the restaurant, she had to sit down after just a few minutes. Her feet were aching and she couldn't face the bridges, other than to perhaps bend over to be sick.

"It's so peaceful here" she said.

"Yes. And only a few minutes away from your friend which is lucky."

"Where are we? It's like a labyrinth of back streets. It's so quiet and dark."

"We are only around the corner from Rialto. Relax Portia, it's not far," he laughed. "I promise. You are safe."

He turned to her, stroked her cheek and without any resistance, she allowed him to kiss her: passionately, warmly and erotically. Using his tongue to explore her mouth, he held her close. Felt his torso tighten as he held her. Pushing firmly onto her breasts, she gasped. Forgetting the world, her problems, Max everything, she allowed herself to be drawn into this intense embrace which excited and warmed her. She felt herself redden with sexual anticipation. Her face flushing with emotion.

As he gently pulled himself away from her, he looked at her. "You really are beautiful Portia. Really beautiful. Your boyfriend is silly. Your kiss tells me everything I need to know about you as a woman. What you want. What you need. What you haven't had."

"All from a kiss" she said. "I don't think so. And what do you think I need?" She put her hand on his thigh. He didn't move, so she moved it to his crotch area and gently massaged him. She felt him grow within the palm of her hand. She massaged him harder. He twitched uncomfortably.

"You need a man. A real man. A man to make love to you. You haven't been made love to in a very long time. Your body's hungry for it. Your feel is hungry for it. Probably more hungry for love than an Italian supper!"

She didn't say anything. Perhaps he was right. Perhaps he knew. Is this what I need she asked? Looking down at her hand and the bulge within his trousers.

"Let's walk Portia, let's enjoy the evening." He looked at her and gave that incredibly cute and cheeky smile. Taking her hand, they walked along the canal and towards some bright lights in a late night café. And all of a sudden it was familiar again.

"You see. I told you. You have little faith."

She straightened her skirt, pulled a mirror out of her bag; her hair was dishevelled from the wind. Her lipstick slightly smudged from kissing. Her mascara had run too. She felt like a mess and regretted wearing so much make-up even though she only wore the minimum. He took the mirror from her.

"I feel like a mess."

He put his arms around her and kissed her. More passionately than before. More meaningful; sensually. He took her hand and led her back into a quiet street. Nobody could see them. He put a hand on her breast then massaged it. She felt an ache between her legs. Then using both hands, he felt her body. Then he pulled back and stopped.

"What's wrong? I thought you found me attractive."

"I do. Very much so but… hey, don't tell Roberto but… this isn't right. I like you, like you very much but perhaps not tonight."

"Are you being old-fashioned? That's a big surprise Giannini. After all those insinuations."

"No. But you're lonely and I don't know what you want. I don't take advantage. Even though it is very tempting."

"Maybe I'm taking advantage of you?"

He lifted her dress up and putting his hand behind her back, he unclipped her bra in one quick movement. Lifting up the cups, he used both hands to touch and caress her breasts.

She felt his hand touch her leg, then slowly glide up her leg, between her legs, under her skirt, towards her thighs, touching her. She reached down and touched him too. He felt quite powerful between his thighs. He was firm and his dimensions sexually excited her. She could hear some people approaching, the noise of their shoes on the cobbled pavement alerted them to the presence of strangers. They stopped. He pressed himself up against her so nobody could see some clothes had been loosened.

"Do you want to make love?" he asked.

"What here. Like this? We were lucky just now. I think I need to go back. I've drunk too much wine. I'm being silly."

He grabbed her hand and they walked down a few back streets and to Rio di San Salvadore. A boat had been tied up to a post. Nobody was in sight. "Is this yours?" she asked.

"You ask too many questions." He looked around, nobody could see them so they quickly got in and put the cover over their heads.

She was aroused and a long way from home. Who would know? And so much in the mood to make love. It felt very private in the boat, cosy and safe.

"If not, I'll stop," he whispered. "But I don't want to. You can feel what's happening to me. There's no denying I want you but..."

"But nothing…" Tilting her head back, he kissed the nape of her neck, gently licked her ear, and then circled the lobe with his tongue. He parted her legs then positioned himself between them. Still wearing their clothes he rubbed up against her as if in the act of making love. She felt his bulge pressed between her thighs. It felt so nice. He was fit and lithe; he pushed and rubbed himself; despite them being fully clothed, she felt herself have a gentle but comforting orgasm.

Pulling himself away from her, he lowered the zipper of his jeans and undone the button. "Do you want me?" he asked.

"Yes Giannini. You know I do." He took off his shirt and bent down, placing it underneath her buttocks. The cover over the boat had slightly dislodged and allowed some light into the boat and more leverage with height. His chest was quite hairy but not too much. Enough to look manly but without being unattractive.

He took out a condom from his back pocket, then removed his jeans. She watched him as he rolled it onto his penis.

"Open your legs Portia. Let me look at you. Let me see you properly." She slowly parted her thighs as he positioned himself strategically above her. He was hard and his phallus looked large and proud. Carefully he entered her, moving gently at first whilst her folds engorged him.

She felt as if she embraced heaven's ecstasy and was at the doorway to paradise. His movements were rhythmic and sensual: "You're beautiful Portia."

But she barely heard him. Passions stirred deep inside; tensions slipped away from her mind and body; every movement was like a love probe that struck at the very core of her being. His movements became stronger, his breathing was deeper, perfectly timed with his movements and erotic sway. As he moved deftly in and out of her, she gasped then felt the mounting passions take over her entire being.

He knew how to gauge his own emotions, his own sexual pleasure whilst balancing it with her response, so their orgasm would be simultaneous and strong. Timing her gasps with his excitement, he pushed deep inside of her, massaging her inner walls with quick, agile movements that excited and stimulated. Every point of pleasure was gently manipulated to cause maximum sensation. He paused, then grabbed her legs, gesturing her to wrap them around his body so she would be even more exposed. She clenched her legs around him.

She closed her eyes and concentrated on her feelings. She held onto his body as he rode her… So hard, then faster, faster until the world was a blur, her body a firework that was fit to explode. As she orgasmed she heard him let out a sigh of pleasure.

He remained still as he ejaculated and moaned; his face was contorted with extreme emotion. His eyes closed as his head faced downwards as he concentrated on the powerful surge of energy that had consumed them both. Rolling off the condom he threw it overboard. He hoped it would sink from the weight inside it.

"You were wonderful." He looked at her and smiled. Relaxed, elated, pleasured and content.

"And so were you. I think we both needed that. You were tight and exquisite. I enjoyed feeling you come."

They lay together in blissful silence. Portia cuddled up to his body. He covered her with a blanket then removed the top from the boat. "Do you think aliens have been watching us?" he asked.

"I don't know. Alien voyeurs?… Who knows. But only if they could see through covers!"

"Who cares? But we certainly showed them how it was done!"

They got dressed and climbed out of the boat. Giannini put the cover back on and tied it up.

"That was special Portia." She frowned. "No, I mean it. That was very special. You're sensitive and gentle."

"We hardly know each other."

"We've made love Portia. And perhaps a bit quick, but sometimes, these things happen. The moment takes you and you take it. We're adults. But it wasn't sordid. It felt nice. You felt nice. Your kisses, the way you breathe when you're excited. You made me feel good."

"I made you feel good. A strange comment."

"No. You made me feel good. I don't know how else to say it. I hope that I made you feel the same."

They silently walked back to Celeste's apartment, holding hands and pensive. Portia had never known a first encounter to have felt so powerful; almost as if her world had been shaken. An intimate encounter with a stranger, she barely knew him but... She felt as if they had known each other a lifetime. Had he awoken her from a deep sleep?

Portia knocked quietly in case she awoke Francois. Giannini kissed her head as they waited for the door to be answered.

Celeste's face was red with anger. As she opened it wider, Portia saw Max sitting in the kitchen.

Chapter 7

"You didn't tell me you were coming. I mean not today...." Portia said in shock.

"Who are you?" Max asked Giannini.

"Does it matter" he replied. "But I think I can guess who you are."

"You're bloody right you can. Now fuck off away from my girlfriend."

"Portia. What would you like?" Giannini asked her, ignoring Max.

"I think you'd better go."

"Only if you say so." He bent over towards her ear. "But I think your boyfriend's a shit. You can do better… If you need me, the bar where we met."

"What's your surname."

He laughed. "I own the bar."

Max had started shouting at Celeste. Francois had woken up and was crying.

"Stop it. Stop it." Portia shouted. "Max, we're going out. Do NOT vent your anger with Celeste. She's done nothing wrong. In fact, I've done nothing wrong. The only who has is YOU."

"That really didn't take you long did it. You hot bitch."

"That's not fair. I didn't expect you to be waiting for me."

"Oh, so you would have been more careful if you had. You deceitful slut. Just how many have you had Portia? I mean it's only been a few days. Ten, twenty, thirty. Should I look for a queue?"

"Nobody" she lied. "Since that certain event in Prague, the last thing I want is a man to force themselves upon me. Like you did." She almost managed to convince herself nothing had happened. She was scared to even think about the last few hours, just in case her pleasure and ecstasy betrayed her lies.

"Is that why you ran away?"

"Ran away. Children and juveniles do that. I left. I left you."

"It was just some fun. I thought you enjoyed it."

"I kept saying NO. I kept saying NO." Portia started to cry and Max calmed down. They sat on a bench on the sidewalk outside a late night supermarket.

"I'm sorry Portia. I'm sorry." He seemed tender and touched her hand. "I love you and probably don't say it often enough for you to believe me." Portia wiped her eyes on her wrist then sniffed. He took a tissue from his pocket and gave it to her. As she wiped the tissue on her face, she saw the black smears from her make-up. Max took the tissue from her hand and wiped underneath her eyes, removing the smudged mascara. It was a momentary kindness that helped her to forget their argument. Also it had distracted him from his interrogation about the evening's lovemaking with Giannini.

"Please don't cry Portia. I'm not here to argue with you. I'm here to try and find a way forward. It has not been easy to get here. Despite it all, I'm here, with you now. Would I be here if I didn't care?"

She stopped but the tears continued to run down her face. "I didn't sleep with that man." Max just looked down at the pavement. "I know you're lying. I don't want to know the details. Just don't confirm if you did."

"But I didn't."

"If we're to be honest Portia, I haven't always been faithful to you and would excuse this one time. I'm in no position to judge."

"You what Max?" Portia questioned. "You've slept with other women since our relationship?"

"Not slept, just irrelevant one-offs. Just a few. Nothing special. They didn't mean anything. So if you have, we're quits and let's move on. I'm not happy about it, in fact I'm very unhappy about it. But I'd rather we were honest. Especially now. I don't want to break up with you."

"We're quits. We're quits" she repeated. Her voice getting louder and angrier. "You've SLEPT with OTHER women since our relationship."

"I told you, quieten down Portia. It was nothing. Just sex. It didn't mean anything so what's the problem?"

"And us?"

"I love you. It was different."

"Didn't feel different in Prague."

"I don't know what happened. I don't know what came over me. I can't explain it. It'll never happen again. I promise. I'm sorry. Is that enough for you? I've come out to fucking Italy to find you. To try and work out our problems. Doesn't that mean anything?"

"And how did you find me?"

"I looked through your address book and found Celeste's address. I had to find you. Would I do this, if you meant nothing to me? Would I? I'm a busy man. You should be grateful. What really matters is you. You. Us. How we feel about each other. I can't bear to lose you. I missed you. Missed everything about you."

"I don't know what I think Max. Where are you staying?"

"I'm booked at the Hotel Bellisimo. Look, let's not argue here. Why don't you come back to the hotel, let's have coffee, talk, perhaps make love?"

"Let's not."

"I'm sorry Max. Today has been too much for me. I just need to spend the rest of my evening alone." Getting up she started to walk away. How could she possibly have sex with two men in one evening? She felt disgusted with herself and began to regret what had just happened with Giannini. But when she thought about him, how he made her feel, how he made love... It felt tender.

"Let's talk Portia."

"I'll call you tomorrow" she replied then carried on walking without looking back.

When she returned to the apartment, Celeste had gone to bed. Francois was sleeping with her and they looked very cosy, cuddled up together. Francois was sucking his thumb, Celeste looked peaceful. She didn't want to wake them even though she felt desperate to discuss the evening's events. It would have been so selfish to wake her up, but she wished that Celeste sensed her standing in the doorway. But Celeste didn't awaken. If she did, she hid it well.

Going into the bathroom, she ran the hot water. When the bath looked full, she climbed in and laid back. She thought about Giannini and how exquisite it had been. She thought of Max, their past, their present situation, their potential future. Did he wonder whether she had been unfaithful before? She had never realized he couldn't be trusted. Perhaps she had suspected it but now her fears had been confirmed. But wasn't she a hypocrite? Look what she had just done. But it was the first time and in extenuating circumstances. She hadn't planned it. How could she possibly consider one night compared to a relationship that had been developed over many years.

Closing her eyes, she tried to make sense of the complicated situation. Or perhaps she made it complicated. She felt so confused. Putting her head under the water, she let her hair float in the water. She pretended she was in a lagoon somewhere. She always felt safe and secure in water. She pretended to be somewhere remote where nobody would find her. Oblivious, obscure, unknown and in hiding. Where nobody could pressure her, have expectations or demands. Washing off the sex with a stranger.

She wondered if she loved Max. She wasn't pleased to see him but somewhere deep inside, she was pleased he had made the effort to find her. Surely that meant he had cared? Perhaps Giannini had no intention of seeing her again. Why was she comparing them? A one night stand could not be put alongside a relationship – a real relationship with Max. Was she really a slut as Max had accused? She felt like it.

Picking up the shampoo, she massaged it into her hair, cleaning herself made her feel as if she was cleaning off the dirt and confusion. As if she was purifying herself of bad deeds; bad thoughts and bad karma. She wanted to empty the bath and refill it. Washing herself with shower gel, she quickly showered then climbed out of the bath and wrapped herself in a warm towel and cleaned her teeth.

Somebody was tapping at the door, she assumed it was Celeste. So she unlocked and opened it. Jean-Pierre was standing in the doorway. His shirt was undone and he looked tired. He stared at her, then looked away and went into the lounge. Portia was frozen that her best friend's husband had seen her like this; wet and naked under a warm towel. There was a moment of sexual chemistry that flickered between them. The words 'hot bitch' echoed through her mind. Now Celeste's husband. How could she? What was her problem? How many did she want in one night?

Portia was woken up by the sound of Jean-Pierre and Celeste arguing.

"Why didn't you tell me about this letter?" he demanded.

"So you've got it now. What's the big problem?"

Francois started to cry. He clearly hated it when his parents argued.

"For months I've waited for a response. Anything. Then a letter comes and you don't tell me."

"You have it now" she shouted. "So you got it a few days ago. What's the big deal?"

Portia was loathe to come out of the bedroom but she needed to go to the bathroom and was also very thirsty. When she appeared in the kitchen, Celeste and Jean-Pierre stopped talking. Celeste smiled at her as if to say, *sorry*. Jean-Pierre was holding a letter.

Celeste continued to prepare the breakfast, Francois stopped crying; Portia and Jean-Pierre sat in silence at the breakfast table.

"So Portia. What happened last night?" Celeste asked her.

Jean-Pierre picked up the letter and read it again.

Portia was embarrassed to speak in front of Jean-Pierre. Primarily because of Giannini, Max and then opening the door in her towel. She felt ashamed that she didn't check who it was but how could she have known it was him?

"I didn't know you were due back last night," she told Jean-Pierre.

"Last minute decision. Should have been another week but something urgent came up and my trip was cut short. I missed Celeste and Francois and always come back whenever I can." He looked up at Celeste and smiled.

"And I always miss you too" she said, kissing him on the cheek. "And as for Francois… You miss papa don't you?" Francois waved his little arms.

"Papa. Papa."

They all laughed and it relaxed the tension. The argument finished, happy family again.

"So Portia. What are you going to do? Max was very unhappy last night. Kept trying to interrogate me about your whereabouts. I wish Jean-Pierre had been here. He didn't arrive back until after you had gone out. You would have sorted him out."

Jean-Pierre smiled and nodded and resumed his gaze at the letter. But then he spoke. "Yes I wish I was here earlier. I won't hide how I feel about that man" he said to Portia directly. "Anyway, what happened? Why didn't he turn up when he was supposed to? He arranged to come out, couldn't get on the plane, then appears a few days later. What was that about? Max being Max I suppose. I only met him once but once was enough."

"Who knows?" Celeste said as she emptied the water from the egg pan into the sink. She didn't realize he had been looking at Portia. "

"We didn't discuss it last night." Portia said to them both. "He was angry at first that I had been on a date and then wanted to try and make up with me. The great Maximilian Schultzmann's ego out of place because I wasn't sitting here like a needy child."

Jean-Pierre looked stunned. "Schultzmann. His name is Schultzmann?"

"Yes. Why?" He got up and his chair fell over. Celeste picked it up.

"Excuse him" she said to Portia. "He lives in his own little world sometimes."

Jean-Pierre went into the bedroom and turned on his laptop and slammed the door. He didn't want to be disturbed.

Jean-Pierre spread out his research so far. Mr. Klonensberg was an entrepreneur with a large jewellery collection. He worked with the resistance and helped fund their expeditions by selling jewellery. He also liaised with Edward Schultzmann who had a minor position in the Third Reich. Schultzmann betrayed all in his eager pursuit for personal wealth. He used the army for information and the resistance to procure gems as payment for a safe escape.

Spreading out the images of the jewellery, the panther brooch his grandfather had brought with him from Prague, next to the image of the snake. Both connected with Schultzmann who was the middle man. Schultzmann was Max's father. Why had he never asked why Max was interested in the exhibition and in Mr. Kauff's jewellery shop? Jean-Pierre knew he had been careless and so focussed on his own agenda he hadn't seen the bigger picture. He looked at the images of the jewellery. He picked up the photograph of the snake. *What is your secret?* He asked the photograph.

The clues had been there all along. Why Max was at the gallery? He's a descendant of Schultzmann and he was interested in Lehr. Why had he been so blind, why wasted so much time? And now this letter from Veronika Kubiskla. He took it out of his pocket and laid it on the table. Great effort had been made to write the letter. He read it again:

Dear Mr. Hughes

My nephew saw your website and has told me of your quest for information.

The story is sensitive and perhaps we should discuss in person. Please come to Prague. Do you have the panther and snake brooches?

I would truly appreciate your understanding for absolute discretion

Regrettably, I am an old woman, crippled with arthritis, I can't come to you.

Please call me when you get this letter: + 42 (0) 221 333 xxx and plan a visit to Český Krumlov. I would recommend you organise the hire of a small car.

Sincerely

Veronika Kubiskla

He left the bedroom and went back into the lounge. "Portia. Why didn't you ever tell me about Max's grandfather?"

"Why would I have done that?"

"And what he did during the war?"

"I haven't seen you or Celeste for a long-time. I have only just met his grandfather. There wasn't much to tell until now."

Celeste intervened: "What could we have known about it?"

"He was a middle man. He sold his soul to the devil for money" Jean-Pierre shouted. He betrayed people because he was greedy.

"He procured jewels" Portia interjected.

"What?"

Portia repeated herself: "He procured gems. Procure is his word. He told me he procured."

Jean-Pierre's face was red with both anger and frustration: "The man was a psycho. Max is a bloody psycho. I'm not saying all children are like their parents but in his case there are similar traits. He wasn't a Grade A Nazi, he was a businessman but he sold lives for his own personal gain. And sadly, my family are somehow caught up in it and I don't know how or why."

"Jean-Pierre," Celeste interrupted. "Don't be so aggressive. Portia's our guest. Please. And also my dearest friend."

"Where was he based?" He shouted at Portia.

"Prague. He was based in Prague." She looked at Celeste uneasily. "Before my trip to Prague with Max, we went to Munich to meet him. He's an old man. Honest, I can't believe he did anything wrong. He's a bit strange but he's… well old and foreign. He has different ways. Maybe what's strange to us is normal for him."

Jean-Pierre went into the bedroom and brought out his research. Laid out the pictures of the jewellery owned by Mr. Klonensberg."

Carefully Portia looked through all the images. "Portia, don't turn over the photographs, I have notes on the back which may influence."

Putting aside the image of Edward she stared at it. "This is him?" she said nervously pointing at a photograph of Edward in his army uniform. He still has that same expression even then he's a young man. He seems kind, but then when you catch him sideways, he's different. " She picked it up to turn over but Jean-Pierre stopped her.

"This is why Max was at that exhibition. In Hampstead, when we all met, when he argued with Mr. Kauff."

"I don't know. Perhaps."

"Please Jean-Pierre" Celeste pleaded again. "This is enough for today. Let's just give it a rest and do this tomorrow."

"NO Celeste" he replied angrily. "NO. I have to know. For years I've tried to piece this together. Understanding where I'm from and why? What happened to my family."

Portia fumbled through the images. "It's OK. Let me help you as best I can.

"Where in Prague?" Jean-Pierre demanded.

"In Prague. He was based in a hotel in Na Porici. We stayed in the same hotel." She thought back to the hotel, the feeling she had in the lobby. The room. The black shadow. Max's behaviour. She shuddered and felt sick. She felt herself go white and feel slightly faint.

"Portia. There was a hotel in Prague that was used by the gestapo to interrogate the Czech resistance. Where they were tortured. It was there wasn't it?"

"Please Jean-Pierre. You're interrogating her. Is that your point?"

"Celeste. Understand. This is not personal. But I must know."

"Portia, please" he said gently. "Look at these images, does anything look familiar to you?" He handed her all the images and a box, one by one she looked through them. When she opened the box she gasped, he had the panther brooch.

"This piece of jewellery... His wife is wearing it in a photograph. I saw it at his apartment. He said it was stolen. You have it."

"It was part of a pair. The other was a brooch in the shape of a snake." He handed her a photograph. Both Portia and Celeste screamed in shock.

"What do you know about this?" Portia asked pointing to the snake.

"This is the other half."

"Portia" Celeste interrupted. "This is your brooch. What's going on? What's happening?"

"Where is Max staying in Venice?" Jean-Pierre demanded. Portia looked anxiously at Celeste. "Where is he staying Portia?" Jean-Pierre repeated.

"The Bellisimo."

"What will you do?" Celeste asked him.

"At this stage nothing. I need to make some enquiries first. There are some facts I need to check. Portia can I ask you NOT to tell Max about this conversation and to keep him here for a few days?"

"Of course. Max hasn't done anything wrong. How do you know about this other brooch? This is my life. This is my history too. Are we connected? Are we related?"

"I can't say yet. But I need your confidence now. Just a day or two, I need to be sure of certain things. I need to double and triple check some supposed facts before I say or do anything. Perhaps now we can find out the truth and bring Edward Schultzmann to account for his actions."

Max hadn't done anything wrong. She thought of Edward. Thought of this old man who could barely walk. She couldn't imagine him doing anything bad... or could she?

"One other thing Jean-Pierre. He mentioned English girls. Something about English girls in his past. He was fascinated with my accent."

"This is more important than you realize Portia. I beg you, do not tell Max anything about this conversation. I know you love him and this is difficult."

Portia thought quietly for a few seconds. "Since I've been here, I've had sex with another man. If I really loved Max, would I have done that?"

"I don't know. You didn't need to tell us."

"I know. And it's embarrassing for me too. I know what you think about me. Celeste was with me when I met Max. I am sure she told you what happened." Celeste reddened. Jean-Pierre shook his head.

"You're a grown woman Portia. It's not for anybody to judge. Not my business."

"All my life I've needed to know about this brooch. It was attached to my blanket when I was left. It answers my life too. I must know. I've waited a lifetime. JP – are we close family?" She felt guilty for ever having a sexual thought or feeling about him.

"I need to check some things first. Portia, trust me. Also Celeste doesn't know anything. She hasn't been involved in my research."

"I don't know where you are going and what you are looking for. All I can tell you is that you can trust me. I loved Max and would not have helped you before if I felt it compromised him. But something happened in Prague." He ignored her.

"Celeste. I need you to go to Mestre tomorrow to meet with Signore Marcello Casteluccio. He has a jewellery shop there and is

168

an important contact. I will scan the images to him tonight and ask that he sees you urgently tomorrow. You can take Francois with you. Take the bus. It will be easier. Can you do this?"

"Yes of course. And you?"

"I need to go to Prague. I'm taking the first flight out tomorrow. Do you have that snake brooch?" He asked Portia.

"No. My mother does. She keeps it in her safe."

"Wise. It's very valuable. Portia, please write down everything you know about the grandfather. Everything, even if it seems stupid or not relevant. I need to know everything, even what happened in Prague. Celeste is wrong to say I don't need to know. I do. And so do you." He passed her some paper and a pen.

Jean-Pierre and Celeste went into the bedroom and left her alone to concentrate on her task. She stared at the pad for about twenty minutes before she began to write. Francois woke up and started to cry. Celeste went to his nursery and took him back with her into the bedroom.

Then Portia began to write. As she started to jot it all down, it felt cathartic in its release. Looking at everything, starting from the beginning. How and where they met. The exhibition. Mr. Kauff, in a chronological order she listed all the events and with dates when she could remember them. Then she bullet-pointed everything from Prague: the name of the hotel, what she felt and saw. How Max behaved but sparing the intimate detail of the event in the bedroom. Just the other presence that haunted and disturbed. Everything about Edward, where he lived, what he had said about his duties. The photograph with the panther. Any comment he had made about women.

When she had finished she looked at it. Somehow it was disjointed and it also made sense. What was Jean-Pierre looking for? How would this help his quest? What was the connection with Jean-Pierre, Mr. Kaufman, Max and his grandfather. Could Edward have really been a psychotic Nazi? Would having that photograph prove his involvement and allow him to be brought to justice?

She thought of Max's pride, how he loved his grandfather and if Max found out, what would he say? How would Max feel about this or whatever it was that Jean-Pierre was investigating. Jean-Pierre had asked her a lot. Made her promise to confide everything she knew but what had Jean-Pierre told her? Nothing just bits of information. Should she question him? Ask him what this was all about? What confidence had he shown to her? He didn't even explain why or what was happening. His motivation, his reasoning, why? She felt angry with herself for not questioning him. So keen to tell him everything, compromise her relationship with Max… what relationship she thought.

And then she gave him all her notes. "Is there anything you would like to ask me?" He said as if sensing her thoughts.

"I want to ask you everything… And also nothing. Perhaps if I know more, I won't want to help you. Only to say with whatever has happened, Max hasn't done anything wrong. He can't be responsible for his grandfather's deeds. And you are not his judge and jury."

"No I'm not and he doesn't deserve your loyalty. I'm just trying to find out who and what I am. My true birth right." He took the paper and quickly read through it. "I must know. Portia. I feel you understand." He was clearly unsure about the next thing he was about to say. "Would you be prepared to go back to Munich to get that photograph? We need to know what he has done, what was stolen and what should be returned. Edward owes a lot of people."

She hesitated: "I.. I don't know."

"Don't answer me now. Think about it. Tell me your decision tomorrow. I will respect what you decide, I know I ask too much. The photograph will unlock who and what I am. What Francois is and his heritage too. Yours as well. Please think carefully and tell me when you're ready." He went back into the bedroom.

Portia took a quick shower and went to bed. Albeit she didn't sleep. If she hadn't passed him the paper, she may have had second thoughts. She was glad the decision was instantaneous. No further decisions needed to be made. It was out of her hands now. Tomorrow would be another day, she would try and rest, wake up fresh and with sensitivity to whatever would happen next. Despite Jean-Pierre's manner she liked him. He was a good man and Celeste was lucky. Then Portia cried herself to sleep; feeling barren and alone. Celeste had everything and she was so happy for her; but unhappy for herself. Would she go back to Munich? She would think about it tomorrow but in her heart, the decision had already been made. Jean-Pierre needed to know his background but more importantly, so did she…

Silently she prayed for a devoted husband and children. A good and kind man; wealth didn't matter. How silly she had been to have persevered in a relationship which had all the wrong foundations; how she had laboured and convinced herself that financial security was the most important aspect. That she should follow in her mother's footsteps.

Her date and wanton sex with Giannini had been mind-blowing. The best sex ever; she felt invigorated and alive. Nothing else mattered – even the stupid fact that her shoes hadn't matched her dress! She cried for her stupid stubbornness, she cried because she had been so wrong, then she mourned all those wasted years because she had an agenda. Because she thought she knew what she wanted. Only to discover that what she wanted was a materialistic illusion that was meaningless. What was the point if there wasn't love.

Chapter 8

"Portia, you need to get out for a few hours. Why don't you come with me to Mestre. We can get a coach from the bus station at Piazzale di Roma. Remember, it's where you came into on your first day. We can grab some lunch."

"I don't know. I… Wouldn't you prefer that I stayed here with Francois?"

"No. He will come with me."

"You mean you don't trust me?"

"No that's not the case, although you don't have much experience with children!"

"So there you go. I'm sure I'd be fine."

"Francois comes with me. You sort yourself out. Enjoy the free time on your own."

Jean-Pierre had been on the phone most of the morning, had booked his flight to Prague and already left for the airport.

Celeste prepared them a quick breakfast, then packed up a bag with food for the journey.

"And you, little Francois, your baggage weighs more than you do!" she teased, then gave him a hug. "You know Portia, when the day's just awful, a special hug from a child makes everything worthwhile."

"Does that mean I can have a hug too?" She extended her arms to pick up Francois who then wrapped himself around her body. He was unusually quiet, seemed lost in his own thoughts.

"Also, you're in a confused place. You need some time alone. Whether you go back with Max or you don't, you need to make up your own mind. You know I don't like him but at this time, that could influence your decision. Then you'd blame me if you had regrets."

"Not at all. I'll call him, meet him for coffee or lunch or something. If we need to be alone to discuss something, I'll go to his hotel. I won't bring him here."

"Promise me that Portia. I wouldn't want him in my home."

Portia nodded. "What do you think Jean-Pierre's going to do?"

"I don't know. He's been obsessed with finding out his family's story. I never knew those brooches were a pair. I couldn't believe it either when I saw it. Am wondering if it's because of me that my nearest and dearest are obsessed with diamond brooches!"

"All this time."

"He didn't share. Didn't think I was interested. Nothing's a coincidence. It's why we were all in Hampstead on that night. Well not Jean-Pierre but I found out he'd been to the exhibition the day before we did. If we'd planned to go the day before, we'd have all met then. But destiny is what it is and we met him in the gallery. It was all meant to be."

"Perhaps."

"Francois can be crying and he doesn't hear. I can be calling out and he doesn't hear. The sooner this is all settled, the better. Leave the past where it is, sometimes it's better that way. I've always said that. There are some things which we don't need to know, whatever happened doesn't affect today and our lives now, so why ask questions?"

"It's important to him Celeste. He needs your support. I for one, really understand."

"Maybe I'm less tolerant because I've heard it all before from you. He has my support. I don't tell him how I really feel. He should concentrate on his son, not his dead grandparents, assuming they're dead."

Portia took the pram from Celeste and pushed it. Celeste walked beside them, repeatedly checking her new white bag ensuring she had everything she needed. Did she have his drinks, some food for the journey, nappies and all the other essential accessories?

"I loved this bag when I bought it but you know what? It's too big. I thought it would be so practical but in reality, it's worse than a bag that's too small. I can't find a thing." She put both hands into the bag as she rummaged around. "Ah, there we go" and she brought out his little red car.

He sat quietly in his pushchair, holding his toy. Facing the direction he was being pushed, he just looked in front of him, sometimes, he would move his head from side to side. He seemed to be enjoying the ride. They were early so went to one of the cafes for a snack. Francois drank his bottle of milk, then had some water from this Tommy Tippee cup. A cute little blue beaker. He waved it up and down a small stream of water escaped from the holes at the top. He smiled but not a full smile. Just a brief lapse of attention from what was really bothering him. What was really on his mind? For a second he looked like a baby again; Celeste and Portia smiled at him.

"You know Francois is my favourite little man."

"I think he's mine too – and you know how many I've had!" And they laughed. Francois joined in their merriment.

"I can't wait to be a mother Celeste. Like you. To have my own husband and children."

"And do you think Max is the one? Despite whatever it is that's in his background."

"I don't know. I thought he was and wanted him. For so long I was desperate for him to propose. I can't tell you how many pregnancy tests I've had. How many times I cried when they were negative. Now I don't know."

"Why?"

"Because of Giannini."

"Oh come on Portia. He was a one-night stand. And trust me, Italians are very good at one night stands… Have you heard from him?"

"No. He told me where I could find him."

"And?"

"And somehow it is, what it was. A one night stand but at that moment, everything became clear."

"So why don't you follow it up?"

"Because in my mind, it's something special. If I go to the bar and see him chatting up other tourists, it'll ruin my memory of him. Bit like Shirley Valentine when she goes back to the bar and hears Tom Conti say 'you think I want to make fuck with you'."

"And if he's happy to hear from you and wants to take things further. And doesn't need 'his brother's boat'?"

"Men who score on the first night, don't want to take things over. What's left?"

"Not always Portia. Although perhaps shagging on the first night was not a good idea."

"Shaaaggging" Francois repeated.

"Whoops" Celeste said as she laughed.

"Shaagggginggg" Francois said again, and the young couple at the next table laughed as well when they looked at Francois.

"I think that perhaps your son is a parrot" the young man said.

"Naughty word Francois. Don't say it again."

"Shagggginnnnggg" he said with a big grin.

"Here, have some chocolate" and she handed him a small bar of white chocolate.

Portia was serious: "How could I give up everything I had with Max for a coffee and a 'S'," looking at Francois. "But he left me speechless. It cleared my mind. He made me feel like a woman in a way that Max, Max left behind a long time ago. Perhaps it was the novelty, perhaps it was because he was a stranger. I don't know."

Not that Giannini could possibly compare with her feelings for Max, she had been with him for years. Would she want to throw up all that for a one-nighter? But a night that left her speechless. One kiss that aroused far more passion than anything Max had achieved in a very long time. True their relationship had calmed down from its initial lustful state. True, it had mellowed into something more mature and supposedly stable. Giannini was just a fantasy. Nothing more than that. But when she smelt her dress at the end of the evening after their tryst in the gondola, she smelt him, his after-shave. She was loathe to clean it, rather like Monica Lewinsky's blue dress. She smiled. Poor girl. Would she ever be forgiven for that indiscretion?

"You're confused. You haven't been with anybody else for a long time. It made you think." Celeste said bringing Portia back to the here and now.

"Would you ever betray Jean-Pierre?"

"Never" she replied without needing to think. "He's everything I ever wanted and more. I wouldn't risk my family, my marriage, my home for any man. Plus of course, JP is the best there is," she said with a wry smile. "I'd be trading down."

Celeste looked at her watch: "We need to get ready to go. The bus will be here in fifteen minutes and I think I need to visit the Ladies before and also change Francois's nappy."

Celeste walked towards the public toilet and Portia waited outside. There was a queue, so she walked away and looked in the windows of the nearby shops. She hated just waiting around. Distracted by the displays, she didn't see Celeste and Francois coming out of the exit. Celeste was calling her but Portia couldn't hear above the revving and powerful engines of the large buses in the station at Piazzale le Roma. Celeste shouted again to try and get her attention.

Celeste checked the bus stop and could see people were getting on. She started screaming for Portia's attention. The bus started its engine. Celeste started to run towards Portia. She didn't see the bus that ran her and Francois over...

As Portia regained consciousness, she returned to the vision locked in her memory. Was it a dream she wondered? Was it a nightmare? Did it really happen? She prayed it was a nightmare. Opening her eyes, she didn't recognize her surroundings. She was in a hospital bed. She began to cry as she realized it had, really happened.

Max took her hand and held it. He had been crying, his eyes were red and swollen. Attached to a drip, she saw the cannula inserted into a vein on the back of her hand.

"My poor darling" he whispered. "At least you're safe."

"And Celeste and Francois? It's my fault. I didn't go with them... Where am I?"

"The New Mestre Hospital." Max shook his head.

"Celeste and Francois?"

Max hesitated before answering. He looked sad and was reticent to speak.

"Celeste and Francois?" she screamed.

"They are both in intensive care. Celeste is in a very bad way. The child is also fragile. They don't know if both or either will survive. I'm sorry Portia. You must be strong."

"Why are you here, how do you know?" she whispered. She was confused and felt as if her life was a dream, that she was physically in a hospital but her mind and senses couldn't comprehend why, they were fighting it. She was confused, delirious and somehow too weak to think or breathe. She wanted to scream, be sick but couldn't do anything. Her senses felt dead. She felt dead. But she was alive. Why? Her heart felt heavy in her chest, her throat

179

felt locked with stress and hysteria. But she couldn't express anything. Her stomach felt full of vomit but she couldn't be sick. She wanted to turn the clock back but she couldn't. She wanted to be dead but she was alive. Why?

"I was waiting for your call, it didn't happen. I was bored in the hotel room. I turned on the news. It was awful Portia." He had difficulty controlling himself. Portia's eyes streamed a flow of tears. She wished she hadn't survived. She was the bad one, not them. She felt a fraud being alive whilst they fought for their lives. There was nothing fair or right. Francois knew there was a problem, that's why he was so quiet. He instinctively knew. It made no sense. A gothic nightmare... she couldn't find the words.

Then she thought of Jean-Pierre. "Jean-Pierre, her husband?"

"I don't know. I was only concerned about you." Did he know? Where was he? She couldn't focus her thoughts then remembered he had gone to Prague. That letter... Did he know? Was he back? So many questions.

"When you're ready, the police want to speak to you. They're outside for whenever you're ready."

"Just give me half an hour. Ask if I can have a sweet cup of tea and some tissues."

" I love you and thought I'd lost you... what would make you happy?" She paused. Her sickness and upset was quickly turning into anger. She had never seen him so tender. He looked vulnerable and afraid as if he was afraid he'd lose her. No longer macho, shouting or demanding what he wanted. He was quiet, sensitive and gentle. She realised it was over. The love had gone. All she could think of was the debt owed to Jean-Pierre because she felt responsible for his family.

"I would like to go back to Munich…"

Max was confused: "Why Munich? Before you make any decisions, they've put something in the drip to stop you feeling sick and you're also heavily sedated. You've been checked every twenty minutes since the ambulance brought you in."

"So what. I'm alive. What does it matter? As soon as Celeste and Francois are out of hospital, we go. They will survive you know. You know that they will both be fine."

"Sure they will. Sure" his voice was soft. "Perhaps now is not a good time to make any decisions."

"I want to go to Munich. See your grandfather. When they're better."

"Of course. I'm sure he would be really pleased to see us. Restaurant VUE again? Did you like the food? Anything you want Portia. But you're not making sense." He stroked her hand, then took it to his mouth and kissed it.

"This incident reminds me how fragile life is. Your grandfather is old. Max I am making sense. I want to go to Munich."

"You're so kind and wonderful. Anything you want, Portia. I never want to feel I've lost you again. I'll book straight away. As soon as you come out of hospital, we'll go to Munich. And I'll buy you a Louis Vuitton bag. Any bag, anything. Perhaps some clothes from Dior? Anything Portia. Please don't leave me."

Portia felt nothing towards him at all. The bag meant nothing. In her heart she prayed for Celeste and Francois but was scared to face the reality of their condition. She heard the bus screech, she saw Celeste and Francois disappear beneath it. Celeste's hand waving at her. They were run over because she was looking in a shop window… Hadn't she just moved on from all that?

She heard a light tapping on the glass window of the door. Giannini was standing there. He smiled at her and had clearly been very concerned. She nodded to him and then he walked away. Seeing Giannini albeit only briefly, meant more to her than Max holding her hand, being with her, or promising her the world. There was nothing Max could do for her now, except get her back to his grandfather's apartment and that photograph. She realized now it was over with Max. His ways, his attitude, Prague had killed them, killed their relationship. So much death. Everything was a blur of death. She drifted into a light sleep then woke-up screaming.

The nurse put her in a wheel chair and took her to Celeste. Celeste was asleep and Portia sat by her bed and waited. She waited for a few hours but Celeste didn't wake-up. Portia held her hand, begged for forgiveness and at one point, felt that for just a fraction of a second, Celeste squeezed her hand. But then her hand was limp. Portia wondered if she had imagined it. Could Celeste hear her? She sat in silence until she drifted off to sleep again. When she woke, she was still handing her hand.

The nurse appeared and took her to Francois. He was in a paediatric intensive care ward. She was not allowed to enter it but she could see him in the distance. Connected to a life support machine, he looked small and frail. She started to cry so the nurse wheeled her back down to her ward. Sedated or not, there could never be enough time for her to come to terms with what had happened. She thought of Francois and tried to get out of bed. She fell over. Her friendship with Celeste flashed through her consciousness. As children, the games they played, dressing up, when they were separated because they had been naughty. Now separated forever. When Celeste needed her when her parents died. How selfish she had been about Max. She hated herself. Then Francois, Francois. She felt as if her soul had been punctured. Her life's force was wrangled and strangulating inside of her. That beautiful boy.

She rung the buzzer by the side of the bed. A nurse appeared: "Take me to Francois Hughes."

The nurse got her a wheelchair and took her back to intensive care. He was unconscious. Portia cried uncontrollably and started shaking. The nurse wheeled her back to the ward and gave her another injection. She slept for a few hours. When she awoke, she thought of Jean-Pierre. Did he know? He would never get over this. How could he? So unfair, so wrong, so wrong and she screamed. Screamed from the core of her being for her friend and Francois.

Chapter 9

As Jean-Pierre arrived into Prague airport, he was keen to pick-up the hire car and make his way to Český Krumlov. It was going to be a long drive and he was tired from the flight. He was only going to be in Prague for a quick overnight stay and had to maximise his time.

He picked up the small, black Peugeot, checked the map and familiarised himself with the route, then started the journey. He felt on the brink of something big, that at last, he would have those answers which haunted, then he could go back to Celeste and Francois and be the man, husband and father they so deserved. He knew he had neglected them in his obstinate obsession but soon this would be over.

Celeste kept asking him to take her to Florence for the weekend. He should have indulged her. He would arrange something wonderful upon his return. He imagined Francois sitting in his pram. He would buy him some toys. Jean-Pierre was excited they would have more time together; the wait would pay off with an extra special trip. A family holiday with lots of photographs to help them remember their time in Italy. Trying to remain focussed on the drive, he was oblivious to the scenery just the route. He would be seeing Celeste and Francois late tomorrow evening and this nightmare would be history.

After two hours, he arrived at his destination. Such a pretty town, dominated by a spectacular castle. The town square was elegant and despite his not having time to visit Prague, he imagined that Český Krumlov probably shared a similar architecture. Like a picture from a fairy-tale story, it was quaint, very pretty and elegant. Perhaps he would bring Celeste here when Francois was a bit older. Realising he was digressing from his purpose, he checked the route to Veronika's house.

Veronika sat pensively in her parlour as she waited for the visitor. Jean-Pierre Hughes, the son of the baby she had saved. As she sat quietly, she remembered the details of that fateful day in Prague, 1942.

She remembered handing over two young children to a stranger who promised them a safe haven in England. Their lives had been saved but for decades she had regretted her actions.

Nazi Occupied Czechoslovakia
May 1942, Prague

A young couple were leaving a coffee house near Praha Hlavni Nadrazi. Holding the mother's hand was a little boy aged about two years. Coming towards her were two Gestapo officers. The soldiers tried to talk to them but the mother became scared and told the boy to run. An officer took out his gun then fired into the air but the

185

bullet bounced off a building and she was shot. The man went to pull a gun from his belt and the other officer shot him at point blank range. The couple were dead.

"We needed to interrogate them you fool" the senior officer reprimanded.

"What about the child?"

"Kill him."

The child started to scream, he was alone in the street. A soldier shouted at him, took a gun from his holster and pointed it at him. He became hysterical.

She had witnessed the scene, run over to him and calmed him. Then she took his hand and walked away. The officer shouted at her: "I'm not in the mood to kill children today so take him." The soldier then approached the dead couple and started to check through their clothes for papers.

"Please, dear boy. Try and calm down," he was frightened and hysterical. She was with her daughter Janika, who took his hand and tried to calm him too. She put her arm around him.

The boy reminded her of Franz, her nephew, who was about the same age.

"Mama, papa" the boy cried.

"You can't go back there. You can't. They'll kill you. Come with me and Janika."

She picked him and took him to a car where her cousin was waiting for her.

"Veronika?" he asked. "Who's the boy?" She didn't speak but just shook her head. She wanted to get the children as far away as possible from Prague.

"Sssh Not now." Turning on the engine, the cousin started to drive the 100 miles journey back to her mother's home in the medieval town of Český Krumlov.

Veronika thought of Franz, her nephew. Her mother had everything for a little boy. She could look after him whilst she returned to Prague. So many thoughts filled her head as the sleeping child nestled against her bosom. How? Why? How? How? How could this child be saved? Her head spun with the questions to which she didn't have the answers. They drove in silence, both too afraid to speak. It felt like only five minutes, despite the ride being hours. When she arrived at her mother's house, she still didn't have any ideas. Her mother would be angry – her mother would be practical. Despite her being a mother of two children and Janika's grandmother, Veronika doubted her ability to extend any sympathies to a strange child.

"Veronika, what is this? A war, a baby, another mouth to feed. Why did you do this? We don't need responsibility for this boy. It's bad enough we're supporting your bastard."

"Please mama," the parents were shot before my eyes. Despite living in a war zone, the atrocities of war still shocked and horrified. "They would have killed the child too."

They gave him some warm soup; he was too frightened to eat so they fed him. Janika stared at him in silence.

Taking off the little boy's coat, he was perspiring and shaking. Around his neck was a charm. A beautiful brooch shaped like a panther with diamond eyes. She went to the drawer and took out her brooch, a snake. The two were a pair. Then she realised, his parents were also part of the resistance movement. A pair of jewel brooches had been given to help raise money for guns and bullets but now they would save two children. She would be able trace his background. Find out who his parents were – they definitely weren't the couple who had been shot. She had to get the children out of Prague and to England. She had to ensure they were safe and would survive the war.

"We can't leave him mama. We can pretend he's Franz. If we dress him in the same clothes, people don't look too carefully; they'll just see a child. People are more concerned about themselves than looking at others. Franz is safer he has papers."

"Wrong, people are neurotic about information. About strangers. What other people are doing and can they protect themselves by betraying others. Veronika, Veronika. You live in a dream world if you think" she sighed… "Franz is our nephew. We can't keep him Veronika – don't get close. We have to get him out of here, or if he's caught with us, we'll all get shot. You have to think rationally. Think of your family. Or at least Janika's safety. You're her mother too."

Looking at the strange boy, Veronika tried to soothe him: "We know nothing about you little man, not even your name. But I promise to save you… I promise." She fed him until the bowl was

188

empty. He stared into space. He didn't speak. He stopped crying and followed where he was led.

"I'll ask Father Novak; he will find a way to get him to England and away from this place. He'll be safe in England. His vulnerability brought out Veronika's kindness and maternal instinct. It was good to experience those feelings in an era where emotions, love and kindness were suppressed. Also it was good that Janika would not be travelling alone. At the very least, they would be together.

Despite the summer months, Prague felt cold. Perhaps it was all the murders, the Gestapo marching along the cobbled streets, where trams rattled along the tracks; a constant death rattle. The city was filled with death, fear and despondency.

"And this panther brooch?" We may need to use this to bribe somebody. Or to perhaps help us? Maybe that is 'the gift'? Perhaps this brooch was the reason? Not the child. He's just a number."

"His mother put it there for a reason. It's the only key we have to his identity and I recognise it. I will make some enquiries. It must stay with him. It's his only link to his parents." Veronika held the child up to face her mother. Her mother looked away. Both knew she didn't mean her last expressed sentiment. Both women had been softened by the innocence of this little stranger.

"Why do you care? People are being killed all the time. We have to survive. It's about survival Veronika and we need to survive too."

Veronika held him, he looked frightened. She wanted to hold him forever, like this. To protect him from the wicked world, the war, the meaningless deaths of people who had done nothing to deserve such a horrible fate. "We can't become animals because we live like animals mama. This is a child – the future. I won't get close but I want to help him. I will he helping Janika, it won't be too hard to save another."

"Our destiny is the work we do with Jan (Kubiš), Jozef (Gabčík), Marisz Ravoj and the others in Operation Anthropoid. We have to lie low and not bring any attention to ourselves in order to support a bigger and far greater cause than what we want. Or what we feel we should do. We have obligation enough. We're almost there after all the planning."

"WE... mama. I work with them in Prague." She thought of Marisz, Janika's father; she tried to deny her feelings but they were getting stronger by the day. They had made love and she thought that had confirmed their relationship but it hadn't because he loved Stella. "You don't take the risks. I'm asking you now to help me with two children, one of which is your grandchild." They stood in silence.

"You have a bigger mission to be part of the plot that kills that cursed Nazi butcher Rheinhard Heydrich. We can't risk complications because of a little boy. It's bad enough with Janika. These are just two lives. We have to think of the thousands saved through our work."

"Please mama. This child is the future. A future we will not know because of the lives we live now. Give some hope to the innocent. Please. Can I leave him and Janika with you, and then I will return to Prague?"

"See what Father Novak can do to help the children."

She visited Father Novak the next day. He pointed to his office, where they could talk in private...

"This is very brave of you Veronika. Or perhaps more than brave as you risk the lives of people around you. Your dear mama..." he paused for effect. He didn't know about her work with resistance and she flushed. If he knew about that too, he would understand the true meaning of bravery.

"My heart drives me with this decision" she pleaded. "I can't forsake these two innocent children. I look into their eyes; they look confused and puzzled. He wants to understand but he can't. I hold his little hand and something comes alive, even with all the pain and suffering that has now become part of normality. And I have in my charge a little girl too." She felt tears forming in her eyes. She didn't want to look frail and weak or identify the child as her own. She bit her lower lip, looked up in the hope that the tears would just roll back into her eyes. "Please help me?" she pleaded.

The priest was silent and held his hands together on his lap. She noticed the dusty pictures, a crucifix behind his desk. Prayer books assembled neatly on the shelves...

She had known him all her life, he had always been kind and she felt sure, he was protective towards her; especially as she didn't have a father living with them.

"And your mother?" he asked. "How does she feel?"

"She is worried. Worried of the danger the children will put us in."

"I see Veronika. I see." He paused for a few moments, tightened his lips and shook his head. Somebody you do not know, have never seen and know nothing about. Could it have been a trap?"

"No. No." Veronika argued. "It was in a flash, the Gestapo were coming towards them. They were shot before my eyes."

"And did the Nazis see you?"

"No, I turned away. I walked away quickly. I was scared. I was scared for myself, the little girl who was with me and the strange boy."

"And you want me to try to get these two children to England?"

"I will help you Veronika but what happens now is our secret. We must never tell anybody what will happen." He was pensive as if uncomfortable with what he was about to ask.

"No, no, of course not. And you will help us?"

"Yes, I will help you. I will find a way to visit a Church in England with my housekeeper. I feel sure, she will feel the same as you. She is a woman," and he smiled; Veronika felt reassured, relaxed and comfortable. He was going to help her, help the children.

"But my dear, I may need a little favour from you in return."

"Of course Father. "He paused again and looked ashamed, embarrassed, and shy.

"What Father, what can I do? I don't have any money."

"Do you find me a good man? A nice man?"

"Yes Father. You have always been there for me. I trust you. Have always trusted you."

"No my child, that's not what I meant. Do you find me, as a man, attractive? Sexually that is."

Veronika was shocked. She looked at him and for a moment he felt like a complete stranger. Having trusted in him with her most dangerous secret, he asked a question which shocked and horrified her. "Father" she gasped. "Father, please tell me I don't understand?"

"My dear, you're a woman now and we live in terrible times. We all need some comfort, some kindness."

"But Father, I am kind. You know that."

"And are you innocent Veronika?"

"Yes, yes. In the ways of men and women, yes." Why did Father Novak ask this? Surely not, surely not, she thought. In any instant she prayed that his intentions were genuine and he would not expect anything from her. She closed her eyes, she couldn't look at him.

"So this is difficult for me Veronika. Do you understand what I am saying?"

"I think so," she looked down at her lap. She couldn't look at him.

He stood up and sat next to her, gently took her hand and placed it in his. "Would you like to stroke me, just gently?"

Veronika was shy and slightly shaky, but touched his thigh. He slightly spread his legs, his cassock fell between his parted legs. "Please my dear, don't make me beg. I think you know what I would like. I too would like to be shown some love. You clearly are a very loving, young woman. Can you be kind to me too? Kind to an old friend – who needs some love?"

She stroked him. It felt harder. Stiffer. She applied more pressure. "Not too hard my dear." He closed his eyes and started to moan and take short, deep breaths.

"Are you a virgin?" he asked as he opened his eyes. Looking deep into her eyes as if ascertaining whether she told the truth or lied.

"Yes Father" she lied. She couldn't tell him she had an illegitimate child.

"Then please my dear. Kneel on the floor and... I'm helping you to save these children. You know I will help you where parents could not. What I ask for in return is very small..."

Veronika bent down, lifted up the robe, he stood up slightly so she could lower his underwear. A slight smell of genital perspiration wafted from his manhood. His pubic hair was dark, his *testicles small but tight. Touching his penis, it twitched slightly in her hand. "Please my dear, just a few little kisses and perhaps a little lick, like it's an ice-cream, something you like... It would mean so much to me."*

She did as she was beckoned, kissing it gently, circling its tip with her tongue. Then the priest put either hand on the side of her head and motioned her forwards as he gently inserted himself into her mouth. She gagged, it tasted salty and sweaty. At least it was small.

"Please my dear, pretend it's something you like. Suck me Veronika. I have always wanted you and this my dear, will be our precious secret. A life for a kindness. For the children."

"For two children. A little boy and girl. Try and keep them together."

"I can't promise that."

"At least promise me they will be safe."

"I can promise you that. Now suck me Veronika. For the two lives that I will save."

She sucked until he orgasmed in her mouth. She wanted to be sick, pulled away and spat out his manly residue that filled her mouth and was stuck at the back of her throat.

Then she got up, rinsed out her mouth whilst he adjusted his clothing. She looked at him with disgust. The taste of his manhood had swamped her senses. She felt sick, physically, emotionally and psychologically.

"Don't worry my dear. This little experience will help you in life. We've known each other a long time, we're not strangers. And you trust me. This is my gift to you, I will help you and together we'll save the children. You can trust me. Do they have money?"

Veronika thought about how she could give them some security. "They each have a valuable brooch . It will be the key and evidence to their real families, their parents' work and if necessary, access to funds."

Two weeks later, Father Novak and his housekeeper took the children to England.

Her home was a small cottage, overgrowth in the front garden where she clearly had neither time nor inclination to maintain. The door was old and the wood was warped. Jean-Pierre tapped carefully on the door then heard an old person walking carefully to the entrance of their home. A rustic turn of a key and then the door was opened. A short, white-haired woman with beautiful green eyes opened it. In an instant Jean-Pierre knew this was Portia's grandmother. She looked at him, nodded and beckoned him to follow her into the dining room.

She had laid out some fresh juice, water and glasses. The entire cottage felt old, a slight twinge of mildew filled his nostrils when he had walked in; everything looked as if it needed to be cleaned. Also a strong smell of cooking wafted from the kitchen.

"Please help yourself?" she said as she pointed to the fruit and water. "However you have had a long journey so I have made you some lunch, svíčková na smetaně. Beef sirloin with cream sauce and some bread dumplings. You must be hungry."

"Thank you, but I don't want to take up too much of your time."

"There's a lot to talk about. This may not be easy for you. I saved your father's life and I too want to know what happened to him. So please, I want to hear from you too."

"I understand. Do you want to see the brooch? So you can be sure who I am?" He hesitated mid-sentence; it was distracting that she stared at him and with such intent.

"Yes, I would like to see it. Not to identify you because you look like your father. You have the same brown eyes, that same enquiring expression. I just want to see it so I remember that young boy. I had a child too. A little girl. Janika. It was hard to give her up but it was to save her life. It was the same for your father too. Every day I wondered what happened. I prayed for them both."

Jean-Pierre took out the photograph of Edward Schultzmann, the panther brooch and laid them both on the table.

"Please Veronika. May I call you Veronika? She nodded. "What do you know?"

She looked at the photograph of the German soldier and her face contorted with anger. She shook her head and thinned her lips. "Bastard. Bastard" she muttered under her breath.

Jean-Pierre passed her a tissue. "Here Veronika. I'm sorry to be upsetting you."

"I cry a lot. I cry for what I had, what I lost, what I never knew and how this war destroyed the people I loved." She tried to regain some composure. "Please Jean-Pierre, let us eat and tell me your good news first. It will be so much easier to take what will be difficult, if I can enjoy and listen to what happened to you." She slowly got up from the seat, went into the kitchen and brought back two plates piled high with food and filled his glass with wine.

"To Life Jean-Pierre. And to your father and my daughter."

Jean-Pierre told her about his father, that sadly, he had a difficult marriage with his mother; she left when he was a child to live with one of her many lovers. He then showed Veronika a photograph of Celeste and Francois. She commented that Francois also looked like his grandfather when he was a child.

Veronika told him of her relationship with Marisz and the daughter she had to give up. The only way the children could be identified would be with the brooches.

"How is your father?"

"He still lives in England. He has a girlfriend and is content. The older he gets, the younger his girlfriends." She was pleased and smiled. "He's alive and happy. More is just a bonus."

"What happened Veronika?" he asked as he laid the photographs of his family on the table.

"I was in Prague, a young couple had just left a coffee shop. They looked nervous, kept looking over their shoulder. Some Nazis approached them; I just happened to be walking past at the time when they were shot. At the time I thought they were his parents. I found out later, they were not."

"And how did you get my father to England."

She hesitated before replying, clearly remembering the detail that secured safe passage. "I went to Father Novak, he's dead now. I asked for his help. He managed to get your father and my daughter out of his Hell and to England. Through his connections with the Church, he found two childless couples. They took one child each. Until recently, I thought she had died. Father Novak told me she didn't survive the journey. For a lifetime I have mourned a child."

"Then what happened."

"When Father Novak was dying he asked for me. I saw him. He told me the truth. My daughter, Janika was desperately unhappy, the family they placed her with were cruel. They tormented her. It... it affected her mind. She never found love but later in life, had a relationship with somebody. She became pregnant but her health or her mental state was affected by the birth. I heard she committed suicide."

"Please stop if this is too painful."

"No. No. If you have seen that snake brooch you must know my grandchild. Father Novak told me my granddaughter was adopted by a wealthy and kind couple. If she was happy, that would be good enough for me. I thought it better to spare her pain and to enjoy a better life in London with her new family. If she has that snake brooch, she is my family."

"She is definitely your grandchild. You don't need evidence. She has the same colour eyes. The same shade of green, very unusual."

They sat in silence, Veronika was shaking, too sad to cry. There were no words to express both delight and grief. When she was ready, she continued. "Janika had been told I was shot. Father Novak was scared in case anybody realised the connection between the church and resistance. He couldn't leave any trace. So cruel. So cruel. My poor Janika. My poor baby."

"And my father's parents. Who were they? What happened to them?"

"How well do you know your history? Have you ever heard of Operation Anthropoid? It was the assassination attempt on Rheinhard Heydrich." She explained what happened and that she had helped. "Your mother was a young English woman working with the Czech Resistance. Did you know they trained in England? It was always a better prize when a beautiful woman with an English accent was captured."

"No. I didn't know."

"She was captured and tortured. Your father was also in resistance. They were betrayed. To keep you safe, another couple posing as your parents, were on the way to the station when they were shot. This is what I witnessed. I took your father and organised his safe passage to England through Father Novak. Your grandmother's name was Sarah. I don't remember her surname. She was a brave and courageous woman. A fighter. She was told you had got out. She was tortured but at peace when she died. She knew you were safe. Your father's name was Yacob Worvoski and was Polish."

"What happened to him. My father."

"He was caught and shot in 1944. Your parents were very much in love. You meant everything to them. They wanted to make Prague, their homeland, safe for your father. . This was their dream. This was all of our dreams. We wanted to make Prague safe for our children."

Veronika and Jean-Pierre sat in silence as they drank some water.

"Did you know them?"

"No. We were different factions within the resistance. The man I was involved with knew them. I knew people who worked with them. Your mother was a very determined woman."

Jean-Pierre felt his mobile phone vibrate. He was annoyed with himself that he had forgotten to turn it off. He didn't want to stop the flow of the conversation by checking his phone. Nothing was more important than the conversation he was having now. He put his phone back in his pocket.

"Edward Schultzmann's wife wore this panther brooch. There is a photograph, I am trying to get it. Do you know anything about this?"

"Because he had the brooch" Veronika replied. "It was valuable so we stole it. The same jewels went around and around.

The Nazis had them. We stole them and sold back for weapons or safe passage."

"If only you knew how much of my life has been haunted by not knowing. Not understanding how and why?" He felt regret for the loss of years. "And these young men?"

"Betrayed and killed. Difficult to explain a time so dangerous, where humanity is irrelevant and impossible to find. Dark times with very dark people. Evil people who wanted to dominate the world. People who would do nothing for nothing. No humanity, no kindness, just exploitation, murder and betrayal. This is such a beautiful place, but the cobbled stones have been wet from the blood of the people who have been murdered, laid in their own blood. Left to die. My nightmares are filled with the scenes of my early youth."

"Do you have a photograph of my parents?"

"No. Please tell me about my granddaughter?"

He wondered what to tell her. "Her name is Portia."

"From Shakespeare. How ironic. And you now live in Venice. A further irony? And does she have three suitors?"

"I'm sorry. I didn't study Shakespeare. I couldn't possibly know."

"A Merchant of Venice. But never mind."

"But I'm the one currently living in Venice with my wife and son, Francois."

"Can you bring Portia here to me? It would make an old woman very happy to see her grandchild. Could you do this? Would she come?"

"I will ask her. I'm sure she will once she knows her story." He wondered if he should tell her about Max but decided not to. Max would be out of Portia's life very soon. In fact the sooner, the better.

Jean-Pierre smiled and felt very grateful to be alive. He felt his mobile phone vibrate again from deep inside his jacket pocket. It was annoying him; he wanted to throw it out of the window. Then he felt a single vibration as he received a voicemail message. He would look at it later he thought. It could wait.

"Did you ever marry Veronika?"

"No. I couldn't find it in my heart to love again. It was too difficult. I'd been broken by circumstance. Broken by innocence I was never allowed to have. I couldn't trust anymore; I felt that all love would end in tears or death. It took me too many years to recover from such pain. Also giving away Janika was too painful. I couldn't do that again." They finished their food in silence as they contemplated the power of the conversation. Jean-Pierre looked around her house, it was humble.

He would write to her, she wouldn't wait too much longer. Hopefully Portia would be on her way to Munich for the picture and when she returned, he would come back to Prague with her.

His phone vibrated again. He ignored it. Then it rung again straight after. It was annoying him but he tried to hide his anger. In the company of such a wonderful woman, he could not show her disrespect by bringing out his phone. Again, he felt the single vibration of a voicemail message or text.

Once he had that image, his quest would be complete. What mattered was the truth, understanding what happened and to also tell his father. His father had shut out this void in his life, perhaps if he knew the people who had risked their lives, might give more value to it. Jean-Pierre was glad to be alive. Glad and happy to be blessed with a good life, a wonderful family and to be safe. Against all odds, his family had survived and secured their blood through their following generations. It had not been in vain.

As he left the house, he kissed Veronika on both cheeks. She held his face and stared at him. "Please do tell me that although I only knew your father for a few days, I loved him. Do you think that he too might come to Prague?"

"I will ask him Veronika. He owes you that," and he smiled. As he walked towards the car, he looked back over his shoulder. She was still standing in the doorway. She was smiling and looked radiantly happy. She waved, then hobbled back into the house.

Getting into the car, he checked his route back to Prague. His phone rang again; he took it out of his pocket and looked at the number. It was a number in Prague. Who could be ringing him from Prague? He didn't know anybody. Then another voicemail message. He drove around the corner, parked and checked his messages.

The call was from the British Embassy in Prague asking him to urgently return his call. He wondered why. Perhaps he needed a visa. He felt annoyed with himself, he hadn't checked. But surely he wouldn't have got through Passport Control. What could they want? Could he also be sure that the call was genuine?

He didn't want to call back, he wanted to savour how he felt at that particular moment, knowing that after all these years, it was coming together. It was all making sense and his journey was nearly over.

Chapter 10

Jean-Pierre drove directly from the airport to the hospital and to Celeste's bedside.

"I should have been a better father and husband. I wasn't good enough. I shouldn't have been so self-obsessed. I put them in danger. I suggested they went to Mestre. It should have been me running around in that dangerous bus station, not flying off to Prague. I put them in danger. It's my fault. Celeste – I'm so sorry." He prayed for her then asked to be taken to Francois.

After he spent half an hour with Francois, he went to Portia. The nurse spoke to him as she escorted him to the room.

"It's not her fault. It was an accident. You both share a great deal of grief. She was hysterical when she arrived and has been heavily sedated

"Her child isn't in intensive care. She's not intensive care. She's alive."

"But traumatised. We're giving her the maximum sedation and even then, we can't keep her quiet. Please, don't upset her."

"Don't upset her. She's fine. She'll be leaving this hospital after she's stopped feeling sorry for herself."

"I'm sorry but if that's how you feel, we cannot let you visit her. She's our patient too."

She took him to a waiting area and brought him some tea and plain biscuits. She sat down and waited for him to drink. It was sugary and very hot.

He took the photographs of Celeste and Francois out of his pocket. He stared at them – they were smiling and happy. Then for the first time since hearing the news he cried. The nurse sat quietly until he had sobbed every last tear. Then when he was ready, she took him to Portia.

He looked at her asleep, left the ward and returned to Celeste's bedside. He put two chairs together, then put his feet up so he could be comfortable beside her.

Portia walked into the room, Jean-Pierre was startled when he saw her. He let go of Celeste's hand.

They stared at each other, there was a long embarrassed silence. "How are you Jean-Pierre?"

"I'm... I'm... fine. You?"

"No you're not. You're not fine and nor am I."

"You're alive aren't you. You'll walk out of this hospital. Celeste probably won't. Who knows about Francois? So you must be fine."

"It's not my fault."

"Apparently she wanted your attention. You were busy?"

"It was an accident."

Celeste made a murmuring noise and was trying to turn her head. "JP… Jean-Pi…"

"Yes Celeste. I'm here." He kissed her head, her cheeks, her hands. She was weak and almost lifeless.

"Francois? Where Francois?"

They hesitated and didn't know what to tell her. Portia stroked her head. "He's fine, he survived. He'll be OK." Tears filled Celeste's eyes and she smiled.

"My baby's OK. My baby."

"Yes Celly. He's fine. You saved him."

Jean-Pierre appreciated Portia's initiative. She was giving Celeste some peace. His attitude towards her mellowed.

"Not Portia's fault. No."

"Don't worry Celeste. It doesn't matter. You're awake. You're coming back to me."

"No Jean… I'm dying. Please, please… Portia.. Por…. Please help JP to look after my baby?"

"Of course I will. But you will be looking after him. You know me. I couldn't look after him like you could, so you must get better. Celly, you must get better."

She shook her head. "Don't try to be me. Be YOU. " Then she looked over at Jean-Pierre. "I love you. Always loved you….."

He smiled at her and then she gasped: "Francois" and a tear rolled down her cheek.

Her heart and breathing stopped. The loud beep on the machine confirmed she was dead.

Max read the in-flight magazine as the plane prepared to leave the runway.

"I'm so happy we're going back to Munich. Grandfather is so pleased he'll be seeing us again. He was very taken with you."

"I am aware he's a very old man."

As the air hostess walked by she offered a newspaper and some refreshment. Portia requested some water. Max had a beer and eyed the flight attendant.

The hotel had lost its initial appeal. She couldn't feel anything and what was a wonderful recent experience, now felt dull and dead. She felt dead inside. She had to get that image and get rid of Max as soon as possible. Looking at him, he was like a stranger. She had fallen out of love. Amazing how different somebody looks when you don't love them anymore. She couldn't bear for him to touch her. Making love was out of the question. He was beginning to repulse her. They checked in and went straight to their room.

"You look tired and stressed Portia. Let's have a sleep." He started to draw the curtains. He presumed too much. So she had slept with him a hundred times before. Perhaps even a thousand.

"I'm not tired. Let's go out. Let's go for a walk."

"Well I'm tired. So if you don't mind, I'd like a rest." And his arrogance. She used to think he was manly, slight dominating in a strong and sexy way. Reflecting back on their relationship, it had such a different perspective. It was always about him.

"Good morning" Max said to his grandfather. "Yes, yes, we'll be over at around 1 O'clock for lunch…. Yes…. Yes…. Yes…. It's Portia's idea. We're looking forward to seeing you." Then he hung up the phone. "See Portia, you've made an old man very happy. Want to make a young man happy too?" He pulled down the sheet and exposed his erect penis. "Something about the mornings. Makes me horny. Fancy giving me a little blow job to start the day?"

"I'm tired. It was a long flight. I'm sorry."

"You're always sorry. You're also getting a bit frigid. Can't you move on from what happened in Venice?"

"You met them too. Don't you feel anything?"

"I met them once and they weren't particularly welcoming."

"I'm just tired, probably the stress of it all is wearing me out. I don't know. I just need some time. Look, why don't we have a really nice meal together, relax, perhaps drink a little too much wine and then let's see."

"I can go along with that. But I'm getting a little bored of your teasing. You promise a great deal but then you don't deliver. You're a cock-tease."

"I don't know how you can call me that? I'm a woman grieving for my closest friend. I've been looking after your dick since our first date."

He reflected their first night. On that score, she was right but lately, there had been just too many excuses. He knew that he would be looking for professional services if she didn't buck up.

"OK, I'll book a table now. But please, stop the games. I'm a man and I have needs too. If you're not going to deliver it, I'll get it from somewhere else. There are plenty of good-looking women who would be only too pleased to be hanging off my arm. So it's your call."

She cringed at his arrogance. When you like or love somebody, whatever they say and how you respond to their comments or opinions is very different, to how you feel when you hate them. So he had been kind at the hospital. Was it because he loved her? His kindness was short-lived. Where his fit body was a shrine to sex; she now saw a shallow shell that had no soul and only a limited kindness despite the situation. Was he handsome? No. His personality was beginning to shine through his looks and it wasn't attractive. She never noticed that his nose was just slightly wonky; that his front teeth were slightly stained from too much strong coffee. His clothes were from Savile Row but they didn't flatter him.

His legs were slightly too long and he hadn't had time to get the trousers altered so they hung at the right length.

She went into the bathroom and enjoyed a long, hot bath. Max watched the television, then they went to bed and Portia feigned sleep.

Max set the alarm for 8 a.m. the next morning.

Portia knew this would be her last chance to get the photograph. It was going to be difficult, how would she do it? She would have to make a quick decision as to when the time was right. She purposely wore a jacket with a long inside pocket so she could just slip it in.

They ate lunch at Max's apartment; it was quiet throughout the meal. Edward stared at her, Max ate hungrily. His interest turned to food in the absence of sex. He was stressed, angry and clearly tense.

All afternoon she waited for the right time. She would need them to leave the dining room for just a minute. They sat at their chairs as if stuck to them. As if they would never get up again. She tried not to stare at the sideboard but it seemed to defy her. As if mocking her. She had to juggle so much, getting them out of the room, getting the photograph, dodging Max's carnal invitations. She had to be so astute and ready for anything. It was draining and she was tired. She wanted out of this relationship as soon as possible.

Then Edward stood up: "Portia my dear, vould you like some tea?"

"Yes please." That would be wonderful she enthused. Then she had an idea. "Max, why don't you help your grandfather?"

"Why don't you?" he snapped back.

"I need to pop to the toilet and just freshen up. Then I'll serve the tea," she said smiling at them both. She watched them go into the kitchen. She heard them talking in German.

Quickly she walked over to the sideboard, carefully opened it, picked out the photograph and slipped it inside her jacket pocket. Ensuring that the drawer was definitely closed, she then went into the bathroom and breathed a sigh of relief. It was done.

Going back into the dining room, Edward had put a cup of tea on her placemat. Max was in the kitchen. She went in and whispered: "Max, we need to leave now."

"Why?" he queried.

"I've just started my period, I need to get back to the hotel room."

"Well that kisses away a shag. Why didn't you check your dates?"

"I'm not due" she replied. "Probably the stress has brought it forward. I don't know. I just know we have to leave. NOW."

They returned to the dining room, Edward had started to drink his tea. "Sorry grossvater, Portia isn't feeling well. We are going to have to leave, but perhaps I'll see you again before we return to England?"

Edward looked at her accusingly or perhaps she just imagined it? Suddenly she felt guilty for the theft and wondered if he knew. Was it her paranoia, or was he looking at her bag? Deciding to expel any concerns, she immediately dealt with the situation. Opening her bag, she took out the entire contents, lifted it upside down and shook it. Sitting next to Edward, he looked silently at the contents of her bag. Then at her. "Max, I can't find the hotel key. Do you have it? I think I left it in the hotel room."

"Of course I've got it." Without a second thought, he imitated her gesture and he too emptied his pockets, laying out his wallet, mobile, tissues, home/car keys on the table, then showed her the hotel key. He then put everything back.

"I'm sorry Edward, but I really need to go. Hopefully Max will be over tomorrow."

Edward looked sad when he nodded at them. "Shame. I vas looking forward to seeing you."

They all walked to the apartment door. She put her coat on and done up the buttons. It was far too hot for a coat but in case he kissed her good-bye, she couldn't risk him feeling the photograph in her pocket. At least this way, there would be another barrier between his skin and hers.

"Have you really started your period or did you just want to leave."

"Yes I did" she replied knowing it covered this afternoon and more importantly this evening. He would have to leave her alone.

The hotel phone rung. Max answered it. "Yes. Why? Why do you think that?" Max asked him.

"What is it?" she asked with fake concern.

"My grandfather has had a robbery."

"Tell him I'm sorry" she said calmly.

"He wondered if you accidentally picked up a photograph." Max put his hand over the ear-piece so Edward couldn't hear her reply.

"No. Why would I do that? Anyway, I emptied my bag just before we left. Remember? How could I have taken anything?" Max nodded.

"Do you have a cleaner, or have you had somebody in recently to repair or deliver anything. Because that's the thief. You should call the police and have them investigate…"Then Max was silent as Edward spoke. "OK, it's up to you. Just saying, you should call the police….. (again silence)… well don't then, but there's no point complaining to me and Portia. It's not us (he laughed) so have the police spoken to your cleaner. I need to go grossvater . Calm down… Perhaps if you look again in the morning, you'll find it. You probably just put it somewhere else."

Edward was still talking when Max hung up. "This has been a right shit weekend. My grandfather is losing it and accused you of stealing a photograph. We can't have sex. I might as well have stayed at home." He picked up the remote control and put on the television. Portia went into the bathroom, took out the photograph and placed it in her cosmetic bag. Men never touch a woman's bag she thought…. Her bag was more sacrosanct than her sex!

"Munich has been a complete waste of time" Max shouted.

"No. It's been a nice time. What's your problem?" Portia had engineered a row. Promised him great sex then told him she had a period. Nothing would anger him more than that.

"The very least you could do is a blow job. My balls are fucking bursting. How heavy are you?"

"NO" she said angrily. "AND I MEAN NO! Have you any respect for how I must be feeling right now?"

"Well it's too much of a coincidence. You're in a bad mood then a period out of nowhere."

"If I'm in a bad mood then have a period, perhaps it's called PMT! Do you want proof?" She came out of the bathroom and pulled at her skirt. She knew he wouldn't take her up on the offer.

"No." He stood up and pulled down his trousers, they dropped at his ankles. "Come on Portia, give me some mouth."

She hated him for this. There would be no turning back now.

"How about you… just fuck yourself."

"Well fuck YOU." He went into the bathroom, slammed the door and shouted abuse which she ignored.

Now to make him really dislike her. Plan her exit route, her getaway, so she could rebuild her life without him. She didn't know what she would do or where she would go. She just knew it wouldn't include Max. She didn't need to be spoken to like a whore pulling a trick. He didn't turn her on; in fact he turned her off. She dropped his Daytona Rolex onto the floor and stamped on it. Looking down she felt very satisfied. The watch was broken and certainly beyond repair.

It only took two minutes to pack her things. She left the room, went straight to the airport and took the next flight back to Venice.

Chapter 11

Again she went to Jean-Pierre's apartment. He was never there and his apartment was too high for her to look through a window. She had spoken to the neighbours and knew Francois had left hospital, was able to walk and now lived at home with his father. She wanted to see him, hear his voice. She went at various times but it didn't make any difference.

Holding the envelope with the photograph she wondered if perhaps she should just put it through the letterbox. But then how could she be sure he would receive? She would have to come back. In the meantime and until this was resolved, she had rented a small apartment in Corte Mende near the Peggy Guggenheim Collection. She couldn't leave Venice until she had closure with Jean-Pierre. He had to forgive her.

Two weeks later, still no reply. For what felt like the millionth time, she wondered about putting the envelope through the letterbox. But then he might have moved? If they ever caught up again, he would not be able to retrieve. Should she get a copy? Scribbling her mobile number onto a sheet of paper, she asked him to call her. She would wait at a nearby café for a chance to just see him and especially Francois. She pined for him. Craved him. Felt empty without seeing him.

Jean-Pierre clearly didn't want to hear from her... And she had just sacrificed so much to get that photograph. Perhaps she had been driven by guilt? But she had honoured her promise. Celeste had asked her to help him with Francois. Why couldn't he let her honour that promise too?

Walking back towards her apartment, she had crossed the Ponte dell'Accademia bridge and past the Accademia. She saw a vacant bench and sat on it. She just stared into space as she collected her thoughts about Celeste and Francois. How much she missed them and how empty her life felt since Celeste had died. In the back of her mind, she heard Francois's 'Zoom', saw Celeste as a child, as a teenager, a woman and then as a wife and mother. She could never have imaged a time without Celeste; like a parent, you just always assume they'll be there when you need or want them. But now she was gone.

Portia thought that perhaps her eyes would dry up and that it wouldn't be possible to cry anymore. But amazingly, she still cried. She had to get out of this, find a mechanism or programme that would help lift her from the pain, help her not to forget them both but to deal with it effectively; so she could compartmentalise and hold them in a special place, treasure their memory and not live with the pain of loss.

She wondered whether she should contact Giannini? Should she or shouldn't she? She would just walk past in case he was there. He would probably be with another woman, why shouldn't he be? It was just a one-night stand. In the distance she could hear a vaporetto approaching and hoped it was Line 2. It was. She ran to the Accademia water station and got on.

As she walked past the bar, she pretended she didn't realise where she was. She listened out in case anybody called. They didn't. She walked past again. Nothing. She peeked inside. He was there. Sitting at the bar with his back towards the window so she turned around and walked past the window where he was facing. Walking very slowly she turned her head so as not to look at him but to be noticed. Waiting to hear her name being called... It wasn't.

Perhaps he saw her? Perhaps he didn't? What should she do? She walked past again. Silence. Forget trying to get noticed she thought: "Hello stranger" she said to his face. He looked at her and smiled.

"Hello my friend. How are you? Better now after that incident?" He looked at her face closely to gauge her expression. The look in her eyes as she looked into his.

He called out to the barman: "A drink for my friend here. Glass of wine please....So, how are you? How are you really?"

He lit up a cigarette and then offered her one. She declined. As he took a drag from the cigarette, she stared at his lips. Remembered how he kissed her. She looked at his hand as he closed the cigarette box. Strong, tanned and manly. A man's hand that knew hard work. Slightly rugged, strong.

"I'm fine" she lied. Why bore him?

"Sure? I came to see you at the hospital. Your face was on every news channel. I recognised you immediately and was worried about you. It was a terrible accident. It felt as if the whole of Venice mourned your friend. How is the child?"

"I haven't seen him." He made a confused expression. "I think her husband is angry with me."

"It was not your fault."

She didn't want Giannini to see her crying; looking pathetic. She blinked quickly so her eyes might absorb the tears. She sniffed, and then wiped the side of her nose.

"I'm sorry Portia. I understand what it is to be happy one day, then feel you've lost everything the next."

"So how do you get over it?"

"You don't. You just learn to live with it. So is this why you are passing, because you would like some company?"

"Are you always so direct?"

"Perhaps. But I don't believe in wasting time. If something needs to be said, I say it. Needs to be done. I do it."

"I don't know what I want. But despite you being so very handsome, I'm not interested in sex. Please understand. I'm really not interested in anything."

"I wasn't suggesting that. I just wanted to hold you. Make you feel safe. I was going to suggest a quiet table. At the very least, you need a friend."

Portia smiled out of embarrassment. Not every man was like Max. She wanted to speak but felt too choked.

"Sorry."

"For what?" He stubbed out the cigarette, stood up, put his mobile phone and keys in his pocket and they left the bar, held hands and walked along Fondamenta delle Farine, near San Marco (Vallaresso) station. He had an apartment which was slightly set back from the main road. It was minimalist, stone floors, a few paintings on the walls, a large flat screen television and comfortable sofa. She walked to the large French windows, and if you looked to the left, he had a beautiful view of the Grand Canal. Opening the windows, the air was refreshing. "Can I offer you something to drink? Some lemon and mint? Very refreshing in this heat."

"Do you ever get used to it?" she asked.

"Yes. Like everything, you adapt. In my case, I have not known any different."

He pointed to the sofa, she sat down. Wearing a short summer dress, she sat with her legs tightly closed. He noticed and smiled. "OK" he said then nodded. She smiled. Bit late to put her legs together.

He brought over two glasses and sat next to her. They both drank some of the juice. It was sweet. He put his arm around her but it was uncomfortable so he stood up. "I think we need to be comfortable. Come" he said taking her hand: "Let's lay down on the bed. Doesn't mean I want to make love, or perhaps I do!" he smiled. "But first, I would like you to relax, to be comfortable."

They walked into the bedroom, he opened the windows, and the room had a bed, side cupboard and wardrobe. She removed her sandals and lay on the bed. He lay next to her and he put one arm around her waist, he crossed the other one and laid his head in his hand. They both stared up at the ceiling.

"You OK Portia?" he asked. "You're safe here. Nothing bad will happen to you. Try and rest, relax, let it all go and try to sleep. Sometimes sleep just helps you cope with the things, you can't cope with when you're awake. So rest."

"I am now. May I ask, why didn't we come here instead of the gondola?"

"I didn't know you. Wasn't going to bring you to my home! And anyway, by the time we got back, the moment might have passed. I did not want to take that chance!" He rolled over and kissed her gently on the lips then lay back facing the ceiling. She rolled to her side and snuggled up to him. She felt safe. She brought her knees towards her body as she curled up. He moved away to give her some more room. She laid there silent, content. Closing her eyes, she didn't feel herself drift off to sleep. She just felt as if she was home.

She slept for a few hours, it was dark when she woke up. Giannini was still next to her. Smoking a cigarette, he looked deep in thought. "Feel better?"

"Yes. Thank you for understanding."

He propped himself up in bed and rested his elbow on the mattress and with his head in his hand. "You looked so peaceful" he smiled.

"I felt peaceful" she replied. "Your bed is very comfortable," she smiled and raised her eyebrows. As she smiled, some moonlight shone into the room. Her face looked exquisite and luminous. Her body looked inviting, like a refuge. He moved his other hand onto her body and touched her breast. He felt her nipple harden in the palm of his hand. He gently massaged it; so soft and gentle. A perfectly shaped breast that was just right to hold and caress. He moved his hand down her body, to her thighs and then under her skirt. "Would you like me touch you?" he asked.

She felt herself drift into a world of desire. They made passionate love; intimate and caring, tender but physically strenuous, until they simultaneously climaxed; Portia screamed out in pleasure as she felt the stress, tension and all the upset culminate into a whirlwind orgasmic explosion and within the core of her sensual being.

Drained, satiated and sweaty, they showered together and drunk some water. Returning to the bed, they lie on it, and wrapped themselves in each other's arms. Not speaking, hardly moving, just comfortable and relaxed. Then they fell into a deep sleep as their bodies relaxed from the ultimate pinnacle of pleasure.

Jean-Pierre returned to the apartment. Fortunately, arrangements had been made to pack up everything, to fill the cartons and label the contents. He just hadn't been strong enough to face going there, it would just be too hard. But now the contract was finished and he would be leaving Venice for Amsterdam and taking Francois with him. Francois would never get over the loss of his mother but a new start would be good for him. It would be good for them both. Celeste's clothes had been donated to charity; her possessions were packed in boxes and would go into storage. Whenever he felt ready to look at the contents, it would be available to him.

Approaching the door, he imagined what it would be like to hear Celeste opening the lock. To see Francois behind her, playing on the floor. The memory made him smile; the pain tore through his soul.

Nervously he entered the apartment; it was neat and tidy. Everything had been efficient in the process. It didn't feel like his home anymore. He walked around every room and then noticed a brown envelope on the table.

PERSONAL AND CONFIDENTAL

Dear Jean-Pierre

As much as possible, I hope you are keeping well.
I cannot even begin to imagine how deep your pain must be right now. Celeste and I grew up together. Every memory I have as a

child, includes her. I felt as if Francois was my son too. He was Celeste's child, a part of her, and I loved him as much as I loved Celeste. I miss him terribly and am sorry you have not contacted me.

I have been here various times as I wanted to give you the image in person but you've never been here. I beg you to forgive me. Hopefully at some point you will.

Look after yourself and if you ever need to talk about Celeste to anyone, I too would like to talk to somebody else who loved her.

I have the photograph but was reluctant to enclose. I know that when you're ready, they're important so please call me and I will personally hand them over to you.

Portia

P.S. In case you want to talk, I've attached a card with my new Italian mobile number.

Jean-Pierre folded up the letter and left it on the table.

Ten months later

Portia was enjoying her relationship with Giannini. It was adult, uncomplicated and offered some relief from the stress and upset. She had also moved into his apartment and was comfortable. She liked Giannini a lot and they had started to talk about a potential future.

Max. She thought about him and decided that life without him was infinitely better than with him. He had tried to contact her; she had ignored him. He hadn't come back to Italy though. It wouldn't be too long before a blonde bimbo would be on his arm, cooing and purring at his every gesture. Rather like she had done in the beginning. She thought about the Tiffany gift, no wonder Celeste was so exasperated. Celeste was right. She was making a fool of herself. Why had she been so flattered? Felt so pathetic now.

She thought of Celeste and Francois every day. She also thought about Jean-Pierre too, but stopped herself. She wondered if he had ever received her note. He hadn't called. Perhaps he wasn't interested anymore? Perhaps they didn't matter? Perhaps he didn't care?

The weather was hot and humid, she was meant to help in the bar during the afternoon but she felt tired. That hot, uncompromising heat, like an oven when you first open it, that gush of hot air which makes your necklace hot around your neck as if it could potentially scorch. She took out the mango sorbet from the freezer and put a few scoops into a bowl then sat on the balcony. She had positioned a parasol over the chair so she had shade and a large fan inside the bedroom, was strategically positioned near where she sat. Warmth on your face, icy in your body from a mango sorbet and a fan's cool air… paradise.

She wondered if Giannini would mind if she didn't go to the bar. She was tired and still had not acclimatized to the heat. As they entered the summer she wondered if it could possibly get any hotter. She texted him to say she didn't feel well. He immediately replied telling her to rest. Going back into the bedroom, she removed her clothes, positioned the fan to face the bed and laid down. So calm and relaxing. She had never known such peace before. Life felt good, she was beginning to feel happier. She was beginning to feel alive again.

Jean-Pierre cut short his assignment in Amsterdam. He missed Venice. Francois seemed to miss Venice too. He was restless in Amsterdam and would wander around like a lost, unwanted puppy. He had thought that the canals in Amsterdam might feel familiar to him and give some sense of continuity but it didn't. So he returned and found a few rooms in a Pensione. He had to find some level of contentment and not feel he had run away.

It was small and neat. New furniture, hardly any decorations and with just a beautiful photograph of Celeste and Francois; he had it enlarged, framed and positioned on the wall opposite the sofa. Sometimes he would just look at it for hours, close his eyes, then wake up to the sight of them. For a few moments, he could delude himself she was still alive.

He moped around the flat and lived off savings. Probably drunk a bit too much, smoked too much, but so what? He made sure he could look after Francois and what else mattered.

A new counsellor was due to visit at 2 p.m. His other counsellor was a waste of time. Sat there with a sad and patronizing look on his face. Sometimes Jean-Pierre would not speak throughout the entire session.

He hadn't dressed yet, needed a shower and a shave. Forcing himself to comply with basic hygiene requirements, he went into the bathroom and prepared himself for the visit.

The new counsellor was a middle-aged woman. She looked very efficient, was a bit overweight and wore glasses that were too big for her face. They just stared at each other across the lounge. "Your rooms look very comfortable. Are you settling down?"

He shrugged.

"I'm sorry that I might have to ask some questions that will appear obvious, but I've just taken over your case. Mr. Norchello didn't feel you were making progress."

"We weren't" he replied.

"So, Mr. Hughes. May I call you Jean-Pierre?"

He nodded so she continued. "Are your family supporting you?"

"I see my father from time to time."

"Sorry, I don't have any details," she took out a pen and paper.

"Your father, Francois Hughes. Has he come to Venice to see you and your son?"

"It's difficult for him to come over. I'm not in the mood to visit him."

"And your mother?"

"She left the family home when I was a child. I don't really have much to do with her. She's moved on; has her own life. I'll always remember the smell of her perfume and hair-spray when she went out. I understood later she was meeting lovers. I never liked women who wore too much make-up or were too aware of themselves – their beauty. That's why I fell in love with Celeste. To me, she was natural."

"Thank you for sharing that. I'm sure if she knew what happened she would be sympathetic. Did she know your wife? Has she met your son? Her grandson?"

"No. When I got married, she wasn't invited to the wedding. I was closer with my father; I didn't want to be upset at seeing her. It wasn't worth it."

"I see" she said. Clearly the whole situation was very difficult. He was depressed and had internalized his pain. No family, nobody around him to support. "What about your wife, did she have family?"

"Her parents were killed before we were married. She was an only child." Then he thought of Portia.

"So between you, sadly, there isn't anybody to help you share this grief. You're on your own."

"Not totally. She did have a friend."

The counsellor raised her eyebrows with interest. "Who is?"

"Portia. Celeste's best friend. But I haven't seen her, well not in a while."

"She must be very upset too. Were they always close?"

"Yes. She was there when the accident happened."

"So she too must be grieving?"

As he said the words, he realized that he had been unfair to block her. He realized he had been wrong. She had done her best. The words echoed through his mind and emotions. He had been unfair to ignore her. He thought of her letter, how she had expressed her pain too. She also loved Francois and he had stopped them meeting again despite Celeste's wishes.

For the first time, a heavy cloud had lifted, he felt slightly removed. Saw things just a bit differently. He felt compelled to call her. Return her calls. Make contact. Give her a chance. Because who did she have? Who was helping her through this and her loss? Nobody. She didn't know anybody in Italy if she was still here. He remembered how Celeste had spoken about their friendship, all the things that had happened to them. Even though at the time, he wasn't really listening, he felt angry that he should have listened. Should have understood more about her and Portia.

The counsellor was still talking but he couldn't hear the words. Just saw her lips moving and when she paused to write notes. He stared into space as he begun to see the situation from Portia's perspective. She had felt guilty, had asked for his forgiveness and he had ignored her. *She must be very upset too* echoed through his mind. He was anxious for the counsellor to leave. He wanted to call Portia. To also say 'sorry' – he had been wrong to ignore her.

"Well Jean-Pierre, you must try and help yourself. I'm sure Celeste would want you to have any help that you could. It's still very early days but you had a wonderful marriage and family. Perhaps in the fullness of time, you may again. But for now, try and

229

be kind to yourself, forgive yourself for anything that you feel you didn't do to help her. There was nothing you could do. They were in the wrong place at an unfortunate time."

He stared at her, wishing her to leave. "So this time next week?" she asked. "I think that perhaps, it might be a good idea to have weekly visits. Give you time to express yourself, how you feel about the situation."

He nodded but didn't note the date in his diary. If he was here when she came back, all well and good but for now, he had to prepare himself to see Portia.

Going back into the shower, he washed again but this time properly. He washed his hair and had a clean shave. He swept and quickly dusted the apartment. He took her letter out of the safe and read it again. It was time.

Portia was sitting in the bar drinking a cranberry juice. The number was a local number she didn't recognize. "Hello" she said nervously. There was silence. Just as she was about to hang up a man spoke; he sounded familiar.

"Portia."

"Speaking" she replied. Again a few seconds silence. "Who's calling please?" she asked.

"Jean-Pierre."

Instinctively she looked for Giannini; he was bringing up some fruit juices from the back and couldn't hear. She wondered why she immediately felt guilty.

"How are you?" she asked. She lowered her voice to a whisper.

"I'm beginning to feel OK."

"Do you want to talk? Because I would really like to talk to you. How's Francois. How is he? I miss him. You got my letter? I have the photograph."

"Yes and I'm sorry it's taken me such a long time to come back. I wasn't even sure you were still in Italy. Francois is fine. Well he's not fine but he's getting better."

"I have your number and will text you a date and time. Jean-Pierre. Thank you for calling me back, even if it is months."

"No Portia. Thank you."

Giannini walked over and kissed her cheek. "You look flushed. As red as the cranberry juice" he teased.

She felt compelled to tell him about the call. "That was my friend's husband."

"The one who died" he said with concern.

"Yes."

"And, how is he?"

"I'm not sure. I didn't want to speak here. It was the first time we've spoken. I think he needs to talk."

"So why now?" Giannini asked.

"I don't know."

"And will you meet him?"

"I have something for him. Before Celeste died he asked me to get a photograph."

"What of you and Celeste?"

She didn't know what to say or do. Should she tell him the truth? She decided not to. He didn't need to know the details; she certainly didn't want to talk about Max.

"Just of us as kids." For the first time ever, she lied to Giannini and didn't feel good about it.

"I think the barman said we were out of lemons. I'll go to the local market and pick some up."

"We're out of lemons?" he called out to the barman. "Abbiamo bisogno di alcuni limoni."

"Don't worry Giannini. I'll get them."

He was surprised, she had never volunteered to go to the market before. She gave him a reassuring and loving smile. "Drop them back here and perhaps we'll go out for some coffee and biscotti later."

"Sounds good." They caressed and she walked towards the supermarket.

As soon as she was out of sight, she took a deep breath and stood up against the wall. Hearing his voice. Imagining him talking to her. For months she had wondered why he hadn't called and he just did. She memorized his number then sent a text.

Hi Jean-Pierre . Meet you tomorrow at 2 p.m. Europa Coffee House near Torre dell'Orologio. Let me know OK? Portia

She pressed SEND. A few minutes later he replied to confirm their meeting.

After all this time, she would be seeing him tomorrow. She quickly went back to the apartment and checked the photograph. All intact, all pristine from their safe hiding place in her suitcase. She imagined Celeste smiling at her. She imagined Francois being pleased to see her. She wanted to speak to Celeste for guidance. Would he be distressed, depressed? What had happened to him? So many questions and she knew that this meeting would be difficult.

She felt her phone vibrate and took it out of her bag. It was another text from Jean-Pierre .

Please bring the photograph. JP.

She smiled. She knew she could help him and was pleased that despite it being very tempting, that she hadn't just left it in the letterbox.

Quickly she went to the supermarket, bought some lemons and then walked back to the bar. She was red from the exertions and perspiring from the heat. She gave the barman the lemons. Giannini appeared from behind and surprised her.

"You look flustered Portia. Did you run?"

She laughed and wiped her brow. "No, it's just the heat. I can't get used to the heat."

"So have a cold drink. Or perhaps it was your call."

233

"It's my friend's husband. Don't say that."

"Something's different. Something has happened since you took that call, or perhaps it was that call. Or perhaps the man who sold you the lemons did or said something," he teased. "But you look different. As if you 'av just seen a ghost."

She shook her head in confusion. "No ghosts on the way to the supermarket."

"No I guess not. Have a cold drink. I'm teasing you Portia. You're too serious."

He lit up a cigarette, picked up his phone from the table and walked over to the bar. There was a problem with the pumps.

As Portia packed up her things, she couldn't see her phone. She must have left it at the apartment when she went back to check the photographs. Not sure what to do, she rushed back and searched for it but couldn't find it. Should she report it stolen? She jotted down Jean-Pierre's number then put it underneath her clothes in the drawer.

Chapter 12

Portia sat outside. The Europa was crowded and there weren't any more tables indoors. She wore large sunglasses, her hair was tied back and a simple black dress. She had ordered a strong coffee and bottle of water. She waited nervously for Jean-Pierre. She kept removing her glasses in case he didn't recognize her. Then put them back on when he wasn't in sight.

Pouring the water into a glass, as the waiter passed, she asked for some ice. It was another sultry day and she was hot. Perhaps she should have sat inside but then Jean-Pierre might not have seen her and left before their meeting.

"Portia?" a familiar voice asked. She looked up, Jean-Pierre was standing beside her.

He looked taller than she remembered, thinner and quite pale. Clearly he hadn't spent much time in the sun. He looked like a man who had suffered tragedy. She stood up and kissed both his cheeks. There was a faint smell of his after-shave. She felt embarrassed noticing the aroma, the feel of his chest against her when she greeted him. She glanced downwards to hide her embarrassment.

"You look well."

"You look like a man who's suffered" she said gently.

They both sat down, he called to the nearest waitress and ordered them both a coffee. He offered her one too but she declined as she hadn't drunk hers yet. "Would you like to share some water?" He asked for a second glass.

There was an awkward silence after the brief courtesies. Neither of them knew who should speak first or about what. For the sake of something to do, Portia opened a sachet of sugar and put in her cup. She didn't need it. There were already two sachets of sugar, the beverage would be virtually undrinkable at this stage. She picked up the water instead and took a sip.

"How's Francois? Is he OK? I miss him. I think about him every day."

"I can't say he's fine. I didn't bring him. I thought we should talk first. It's not easy."

Another awkward silence…. Portia opened another sachet of sugar.

"That's the second sachet."

"Actually it was my fourth" and they both laughed. "I feel uncomfortable, don't know what to say or do, so I add more sugar to an already, over-sugared, undrinkable cup of coffee." A waitress brought over Jean-Pierre's glass – Portia handed her the over-sugared coffee. They laughed, it broke the tension.

"I miss her Jean-Pierre. I think about her every day."

"Me too" he replied. "There are days when I wake up and for a second think it was a dream."

"I know. There are times when I want to call her because I miss her and feel it's been too long since we last spoke. But Francois is alive."

Jean-Pierre was overcome with emotion. He didn't speak. Just nodded.

"I don't think either of us will ever get over it. The best we can do is try to manage without them but there will always be this loss. This aching emptiness that chews away at the insides. I can't imagine ever feeling complete again. Celeste was always there for me and sometimes when I don't know what to do, I imagine her talking to me. She helps me make the right decisions; just knowing her still makes a difference."

Jean-Pierre was touched by the way she described the friendship. The counsellor was right in saying he should spend time with somebody to share the grief. That other people would feel the same, it wasn't just about him.

"And so what are you up to now?" he asked. "I'm surprised you're still here in Italy. I would have thought you would have gone back to England."

"I nearly did, a few times, but I've become comfortable here. It's taken a while to grow on me but well, I'm alive."

"Yes, once Venice gets under your skin, she stays there forever." He was talking about Italy but could have easily have been talking about Celeste.

"Did you bring the photograph?" he asked.

"Yes. It's in my bag. Would you like to look at it here, or somewhere else?"

"What does it look like?" he asked.

"You will find it difficult. Especially after what has happened. How was Prague?"

"I have met your grandmother and found out about my family too. Both our grandparents were in the resistance. Your mother and my father had safe passage arranged by your grandmother. She was very brave and would like to see you."

"My grandmother. I… I thought this was about you."

"It has been about us. Our history. It was no coincidence we met. We have shared history."

Portia was dumbfounded. She hesitated before speaking: "I'd like to see her too. What has happened since we last met?"

"All the answers to everything and the loss of my wife. It feels strange but somehow it's now irrelevant. Especially after all the years of searching. Everything I needed to know, I now know but it's… it's not the same without Celeste."

"Is now the time or place to tell me everything?"

"Does Max know you took the photograph?"

"He may suspect but it was never confirmed. Edward knew straight away it was stolen but nothing has happened. I don't care."

"And Max?"

"I don't know. We don't…" she looked uncomfortable.

"Don't worry. You did a wonderful thing for me, going back to Munich to get the photograph, especially so quickly after what happened. We can talk here. We're lost within the crowd. "

Portia took out the envelope and handed it to him.

"Do you know how long I've been waiting for this?"

"And now you have it." He opened up the envelope and looked at the photograph.

"What was he like? Edward Schultzmann ."

"Polite enough, tried to be gentlemanly but there was something obviously sinister about him. I felt uncomfortable in his company. He stared too often; he was creepy. Apparently he had a thing for my accent."

"Yes. He was partial to women with British accents as generally, it would hint at resistance training in England. And Max?"

"Max and he were close. I know Max had his problems and certainly some issues but essentially he's not a bad man. Perhaps he has a problem with women and is spoilt and arrogant. He thinks he's better than everybody else, earns too much money so therefore can buy anything or anybody he wants. It worked with me, for a while."

"I thought you two would end up together."

"Now I see him for what he is, that doesn't say much for me" she teased and they laughed gently.

"It's good to see you Portia."

"It's good to see you too. It's been too long and we could have helped each other through this. It was your choice, you made your decision."

"I need to leave now but perhaps if you would like, we could meet again?" Portia smiled at him and he felt touched.

"Yes, I would like that. How about Friday lunchtime. Let me take you for lunch, or perhaps we can eat here? It's comfortable and relaxed… Did you get my text?" he asked.

"No, I lost my phone. I turned up anyway and hoped you hadn't cancelled."

"OK. Perhaps it's better anyway."

"So, I'll see you on Friday. I'll be here at 1 p.m." They kissed each other goodbye, a brush on the cheeks but it felt poignant.

Jean-Pierre missed Celeste but for the first time, realized that it had been a long time since he had been with a woman. He felt guilty even thinking it and pulled back from her. Portia sensed what he was thinking. "It's OK Jean-Pierre. I'm Portia. I'm not a stranger."

Then she walked away without looking back.

It wasn't an accident that Giannini had picked up her phone at the bar. She looked different, excited about something, happier than she had looked for a long time. He saw how she had clutched her phone and was nervous when he approached. So to find out what was happening, he checked her phone as if it was his and walked away. He had been monitoring her texts ever since.

She had received a message from Jean-Pierre:

I'm looking forward to seeing you Portia. I'm sorry it's been so long for me to get back to you. But at least we're meeting tomorrow. Jean-Pierre

When she spoke about him, her affection was obvious. Giannini knew they would probably not end up together but he didn't think it would be over so soon. And yes, he understood it was her friend's husband but it had now been nearly a year. He seemed as keen to meet her, as she looked excited to see him. He waited for her to tell him what was happening. She didn't. This only confirmed what he suspected. That she was in love with another man.

When Portia returned to the apartment, Giannini was sitting near an open window, drinking a chilled Peroni and smoking a cigarette.

"Hi Giannini" she called. "I'm back."

"Have a good time? Grab a drink and join me. It's lovely and cool out here." He heard her go to the refrigerator, he heard the door close and then she appeared. She looked beautiful. She took off her glasses and her eyes looked brighter, she was smiling and happy.

"So Portia" he asked. "Where have you been today?"

"Oh nowhere special. Just walking around."

"You look very glamorous for somebody who's just been walking. You normally get flustered from the heat. But now, you look like a film star."

"I think it's the dress. Just some cheap dress. I've had it years."

"Well maybe it's you who makes it look good." He drank his beer, took a few puffs of his cigarette and then extinguished it.

"Anything else?" he queried.

Portia thought about it then shook her head. "No, went for a coffee, met a friend, had a chat. Nothing special. Nobody special."

"I see." He lit another cigarette and sat in silence.

"You're smoking a lot Giannini."

"Just tired. Want to lay down?"

"Soon, I want to have a shower and just chill a bit first."

"Sure, I'm going to rest. I need to just relax for a little while."

"What's wrong Giannini? You look sad?"

"Nothing's wrong Portia. Just feel as if I've lost something…"

She didn't get the hint. "Well have you checked your pockets?"

"No, what I'm losing, I never kept in my pockets."

"You're so confusing sometimes. Perhaps you do need a rest."

"So join me?" he asked again.

"Soon. I'll join you soon."

"Portia, you know I've enjoyed our relationship but knew it wouldn't last forever."

"I don't understand."

"You do. And it's OK. Honest. It's OK."

Giannini stood up, went into the bedroom, took off his clothes except his pants and lay on the bed. He waited for her. She had a shower, then went into the lounge, turned on the television and started to watch a film. He went to sleep.

Jean-Pierre and Portia met that Friday, had lunch and discussed Celeste and Francois. They met again two days later for coffee, then again the following week.

"It's time to see Francois. Come back to my apartment."

Portia noticed that Jean-Pierre was beginning to get a tan. He was eating better and his shape had improved. He had a haircut and was looking after himself. Despite the uncompromising sadness in his eyes, he was coming alive again, beginning to look like the Jean-Pierre she remembered.

"I don't know this area well." She told him, unsure as to whether visiting his home was a good idea but she didn't want to say anything that would stop her seeing Francois.

"I'll meet you outside the Café Europa and we'll go together. Tomorrow at 2.30 p.m. We'll just go back for an hour or so. I know you're busy."

"I'm not too busy to see Francois. I miss him. Do you think he will remember me?"

"He definitely remembers you. He keeps saying Porta. He never managed Portia."

Giannini was working longer hours at the bar. He was coming in later and sometimes he had just drunk too much. Whenever he suggested they made love, she felt reticent. He seemed to understand and accepted the situation. She just wasn't in the mood. They were becoming friends instead of lovers.

Portia was wearing a green dress and a green, crystal brooch. Her eyes were accentuated by the flattering shade of green. Instead of lipstick, she wore a subtle natural shade of pink gloss.

"Wow Portia. You look beautiful" Jean-Pierre declared when he saw her.

"Oh, it's nothing special," she argued.

They walked in silence towards the apartment, Portia couldn't wait and wanted to run. As they approached the door, Jean-Pierre called out to Francois. He put the key in the door and she heard a child's footsteps running along the stone floor and an adult's footsteps immediately behind. As Jean-Pierre opened the door Francois was standing there, behind him a young and very attractive woman.

"Francois" Portia exclaimed, bent down and hugged him. His little arms held tight around her neck.

"Porta. Porta." She closed her eyes and wished the world would stop moving for just a few minutes. She wanted everything to stop so she could hold on tight to Celeste's son.

"Portia, this is Francesca."

Portia stood up, picked up Francois and held him. His arms still around her neck.

"Hello Francesca."

"Buongiorno signora."

"Francesca is my housekeeper. She looks after the apartment and Francois when I'm not here."

Portia looked at Jean-Pierre and smiled.

Francois was radiant, his eyes sparkled and for the first time since Celeste had died, looked relaxed and content. He held tightly onto Portia's neck.

"He seems happy with you."

"I'm happy with him." She bent down and unclasped him. Sitting on the floor, she went down to his level and put her arm around him. He cuddled up to her.

"Celeste asked you to help me raise Francois. Because she knew he would need you."

"I can't replace Celeste. She was a special person. A wonderful friend, a devoted wife and loving mother."

"You have those traits."

"But I am me - and I am flawed. Very flawed."

Jean-Pierre sat on the floor beside Portia and Francois. "You can only be you. Celeste knew the real you and that was good enough. I'd like us to go to Prague. To meet your grandmother. I promised her that I would take you there. Her story is a sad one but she is an incredible woman. I honour my promises and it is the right thing to do. I would like her, to tell you, your story."

"So how do you feel now?" she asked. "Do you have your answers? This wasn't about me."

"It was for Francois but that doesn't matter now. It all didn't matter when Celeste died."

"It did matter. It mattered to us both and Celeste understood. She was patient."

"Our diamond brooches had their secrets. A past stained with blood and tears. A history that now needs closure so we can move forward. It's about what is alive now."

She felt hot and uncomfortable; she ran her fingers through her hair, and then shook her head. It touched him. Her neck and shoulders were beautifully curved; the nape of her neck had a perfect contour, her skin looked like silk.

They stood up and in silence looked at each other. A mutual unspoken compromise.

"I'm sorry Portia. It's just…"

"Been a long time."

He didn't answer he felt vulnerable. "Yes."

She took his hands and kissed them. "It's OK. Celeste was my best friend and your wife. I'm not a stranger." She didn't mean to sound so forward but it felt right and natural. Like the continuation of something rather than the start of something new. He didn't argue.

"I... I just need to be held by somebody who cares."

"So do I… By you. I loved Celeste, I therefore love her husband. As for Francois, who couldn't love this adorable child? Who knows what will happen to us but if it's right, it will turn into a love that's right between adults. Love Never Lies - and then we will know."

Francois tugged at her leg. She picked him up and the three held each other tight. Closing their eyes they felt bonded by an absolute love and respect for a very special woman, Celeste. They both knew she would have been happy they found love and comfort with each other. Her family would be their family.

"And now, let's play with Francois."